Who Really Killed
Cock Robin?

Books by Jean Craighead George

All Upon a Stone
Gull Number 737
Hold Zero!
The Hole in the Tree
My Side of the Mountain
Snow Tracks
Spring Comes to the Ocean
The Summer of the Falcon
The Thirteen Moons (Ecology of the Seasons)

Who Really Killed Cock Robin?

AN ECOLOGICAL MYSTERY

Jean Craighead George

E. P. DUTTON & CO., INC. NEW YORK

Published simultaneously in Canada by Clarke, Irwin & Company Limited, Toronto and Vancouver

SBN: 0–525–42700–7   LCC: 76–157944

Designed by Dorothea von Elbe
Printed in the U.S.A.
First Edition

To
sunshine, clear water, and
sparkling skies
and
the kids who are cleaning up the
Earth

Acknowledgments

Thanks to friends in the Bureau of Sports Fisheries and Wildlife (Department of the Interior) and the Scripps Institution in La Jolla, California, for their research into the effects of pollutants on the environment. Also thanks to the Sierra Club, the Audubon Society, and Friends of the Earth for their pioneer work in bringing ecology to the attention of the lawmakers and the people.

I am also indebted to the following journals and books: *Environment*, Vol. 12, No. 1, January–February 1970; three issues of *Nature*, Vol. 224, October 18, 1969, p. 247, and December 20, 1969, p. 1219; and Vol. 220, December 14, 1968, p. 1098; *Science News*, Vol. 90/8, October 1966, p. 272; two issues of *Science*, Vol. 168, April 24, 1970, p. 453, and April 24, 1970, p. 456; *Silent Spring* by Rachel Carson, Houghton Mifflin (Boston: 1962) and *Studies in the Life History of the Song Sparrows*, Vols. I and II, by Margaret Morse Nice, Dover Publications (New York: 1937, 1943).

JEAN CRAIGHEAD GEORGE

Contents

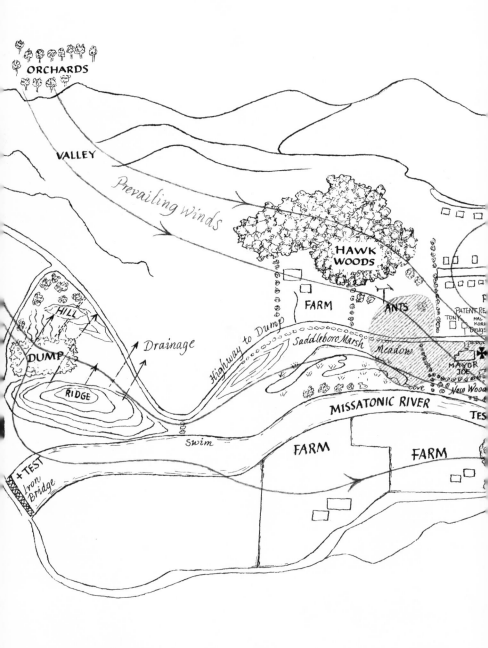

ORCHARDS

VALLEY

Prevailing winds

HAWK
WOODS

HILL

Drainage

Highway to Dump

FARM

ANTS

PATENT RE
MAC
KORR
DRUGS

TONY

DUMP

RIDGE

Saddleboro Marsh

Meadow

MAYOR
JOE

Cove

New Wood

MISSATONIC RIVER

TES

+TEST
*Iron
Bridge*

Swim

FARM

FARM

FARM

▨ *Cock Robin's territory*
✳ *marks the spot where Cock Robin died*

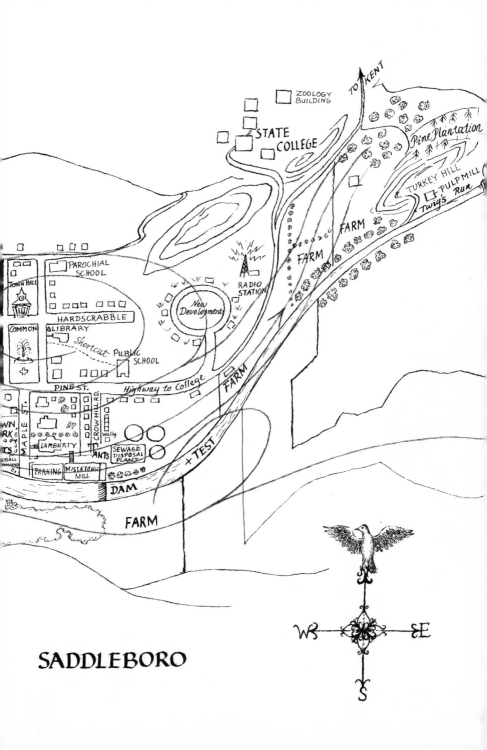

ZOOLOGY
BUILDING

TO KENT

STATE
COLLEGE

Pine Plantation

TURKEY HILL

PULPMILL

Twig's Run

FARM

FARM

FARM

PAROCHIAL
SCHOOL

RADIO
STATION

New
Development

TOWN HALL

HARDSCRABBLE

COMMON

LIBRARY

Shortcut PUBLIC
SCHOOL

FARM

PINE ST.

Highway to College

MAPLE ST.

CROW HILL RD.

Wally

WN
RK
TS
EBALL AMOND
&

LAMBERTY

ANTS

SEWAGE
DISPOSAL
PLANT

+ TEST

PARKING

MISSATONIC
MILL

DAM

FARM

N

W

E

S

SADDLEBORO

1. Cock Robin

Cock Robin lay on his back with his feet in the air. A red breast feather twisted in the wind, his clove-brown wings folded like a dancer's fan. It was seven minutes past six A.M. on the twenty-fourth day of May. He was dead.

Many robins have died without notice by the human race, but this was a particular robin, the Cock Robin of Saddleboro, and his death was a crisis.

At nine minutes past six on that memorable morning the telephone rang in the kitchen of 65 Elm Street and awoke Tony Isidoro, who was sleeping in his room at the top of the back steps. He uncurled all of his five feet three inches, put his feet on the floor, and shook his head. Slowly he ran his fingers through a crop of shining black hair. The phone jangled again and he stumbled downstairs to answer it. As he grabbed the receiver he tripped over his eighth-grade math book, which he had left on the floor by the kitchen door so he would remember it when he left for school. Kicking it sleepily aside, he mumbled "Hello."

"Cock Robin is dead!" a voice exclaimed. Tony recognized Mary Alice Lamberty, the daughter of the wealthiest man in town. For a moment he did not answer.

"He's dead!" she repeated, and this time he asked her how she knew.

"Mayor Joe just called my father," she replied. "He accused Daddy of killing Cock Robin because our mill still dumps aniline dyes in the river. This is not true."

"Why are you telling *me?*"

"You know perfectly well why I'm telling you. The Mayor gets all his information about robins from you and he's going to ask you who killed Cock Robin. I know he will; and I just want you to know right now that if anyone murdered him, it was the Mayor with all his fancy garden sprays."

Tony rubbed his eyes with his fist and shifted his weight from one foot to the other. He was about to say something, but Mary Alice hung up before he could collect his thoughts. He shrugged and went back to his room, picked up his field glasses, and focused them on Mayor Dambrowski's lawn across the street.

There lay Cock Robin with his feet in the air. Several

silver-winged bugs slipped out of the bird's feathers and disappeared into the grass. Their departure was as clearly a sign of the robin's death to Tony as rats deserting a ship are a sign of its sinking. His brow crinkled with sadness, then he put down his binoculars and walked to his desk. Reaching behind a terrarium of plants and caterpillars, he picked up a small pocket notebook and opened it.

The first entry was dated April 29: "A male robin arrived in the maple tree across the street just after sunup," he read. "He hasn't sung yet, so I don't know if he is on his way to Canada or is home. However, he acts as if he were home, for he is inspecting the limbs of the trees, preening his feathers, and looking down on the yard."

The next note was dated April 30: "The male in Dambrowski's yard sang the territorial song of the robin who is home from the South." Farther down on the same page Tony saw that he had made a note of other male robins. "One is singing from somewhere near the library. Also in the Town Park, also on Pine Street."

Tony was keeping these notes for his older brother, Izzy, who had been drafted into the Army before he had been able to finish his graduate-school thesis on the robins of Saddleboro. A few days before his leaving last fall, he had asked Tony to keep tabs on "his" birds when they returned in the spring. Flattered by such a responsibility, Tony had assured him he would do his best.

Although Izzy was eleven years older, he had often taken Tony on his rounds of the streets and yards of Saddleboro. They counted robins, mapped their distribution, and numbered eggs and fledglings. The night before departing for boot camp Izzy had sat down with Tony and showed him how to take notes.

"Good notes are the basis of scientific research," he told him. "If you take them well they'll reveal the truth." He had then taken Tony around the town again, told him to jot down weather, plants, anything unusual or even usual, then suggested he make one round alone. When he came home, Izzy had been surprised by his powers of observation and had told him so with a real pat on the back.

Six months had passed since then.

Tony studied his notes, then went to Izzy's office-bedroom to brief himself for the phone call from the Mayor that Mary Alice had told him to expect. He took out a map of bird territories and saw that where there had been many pairs of robins four years ago, there now were very few. He was shocked. Like all the people of pollution-fighting Saddleboro, Tony was under the illusion there were more, not fewer robins. Since Mayor Joe and his Clean Environment Party had come into power everyone assumed that Saddleboro was a model town where man, plant, and beast were in balance. There was good reason for this assumption.

Joe Dambrowski, or Mayor Joe, as he was called, had been elected to office after campaigning against DDT, automobile exhaust, and the sewage pollution in the Missatonic River that runs past Saddleboro. He obtained funds from the state and town and built a sewage-disposal plant. He also walked to work instead of using his automobile to avoid putting carbon dioxide and lead in the air, and organized the children to find every can in town that contained DDT. These were collected by the Saddleboro sanitation trucks, then buried in wet cement near the town dump. After that everyone agreed that the river was clearer, the birds sang louder, and the air was much sweeter in Saddleboro.

And then on April 29, Tony observed the male robin on the Mayor's lawn. On May 3 the bird was on his way to becoming the famous Cock Robin of Saddleboro. This was when his mate started building a nest in the Mayor's Stetson hat, which he had absentmindedly left on the iron planter on his front porch.

"Providence!" the Mayor had gasped and hurried to the newspaper office to tell David Lowenthal, editor of the *Patent Reader*. He saw the robin as an answer to the Clean Environment Party's prayer. He and the editor had been trying to think up a new gimmick to promote the Mayor in the fall elections. The woodsy-looking Stetson they had used for an image four years ago was a town joke now, and they wanted something fresh. Here it was—Cock Robin in that old hat! The next morning the paper carried a picture of the grinning Mayor pointing to the grasses in his Stetson.

The caption read, COCK ROBIN HAS PICKED DAM-BROWSKI, THE MAN WHO IS RESPONSIBLE FOR SADDLE-BORO'S UNPOLLUTED WATER AND AIR. A story followed that quoted the Mayor as saying he would not wear his Stetson again until the bird's nest was done, the eggs hatched, and the baby robins flying in the "clean air of Saddleboro."

On May 4 Tony decided to speak to the Mayor and tell him about Izzy's thesis, but as he approached the house Mary Alice Lamberty arrived at his gate. She was small for a twelve-year-old girl, but dynamic. Her feet flashed as she walked, her large brown eyes snapped with intelligence, and she tossed her head when she spoke. The only child of Frank Lamberty, owner of the Missatonic Mill, the factory in Saddleboro that largely supported the people of the town, Mary Alice was always so motivated that she stunned Tony into silence when she spoke to him.

He waited by the hedge while she knocked on the door and asked about the birds in the hat. Tony heard the Mayor say that Cock Robin had sung to Mrs. Robin at five-thirty A.M. and had so thrilled the lovely female that she had joined him on the lawn for breakfast. He also said that it took Cock Robin five yanks to get one of his giant earthworms out of his rich green lawn. Mary Alice had thrown back her head and laughed. The Mayor had smiled at her and Tony wondered if the bird was going to end the long feud between the Mayor and Frank Lamberty.

Mr. Lamberty dumped the aniline dyes from the Missatonic Mill into the river and killed thousands of fish every year. The Mayor had publicly requested him to stop this and buy tank trucks to haul the poisonous chemical to the dump. Frank had refused, saying the Mayor would bankrupt the town's major source of income, his mill, by taxing it heavily to help pay for the sewage-disposal plant, and then asking him to buy trucks. The argument was not settled publicly, but the Mayor was so friendly to Mary Alice that Tony wondered if something was going on behind closed doors.

The next day Mary Alice was again at the Mayor's gate before Tony, and again he waited and listened as Mayor Joe came to the door and said that Mrs. Robin had brought mud from the marsh and worked it into the grass like a potter strengthening a bowl. On the third day Tony trailed behind as the Mayor walked to work with Mary Alice and reported that Mrs. Robin had shaped the cuplike nest with her breast. He demonstrated by throwing out his chest. Mary Alice was so fascinated that she called two of her friends who were crossing the Commons and they also listened to the Mayor, who ended his tale by hopping like Mrs. Robin as she leaped from the front porch to the nest in his hat. They laughed hysterically. Having no children of his own, he took this to mean they appreciated his gift of storytelling.

When the girls turned down Hardscrabble Street Tony finally got a chance to speak to Mayor Joe, but he said only, "How do you do, I'm Tony Isidoro. I live across the street from you." The Mayor was glad for someone else to talk to.

"I really should tell this robin story to a wider audience," he had said. "I tell it rather well, if I must say so myself."

On May 7, when Tony crawled out of bed and turned on his radio, he was not surprised to hear an ad for the "Cock Robin Hour—a living narrative by our Mayor. The story of bird home-life as it happens." Tony was listening, as were a good number of other Saddleboro residents when the program began at seven A.M. The Mayor began by saying station WSAD had installed a microphone in his living room so that he could report the events at the nest as they happened. He then described Mrs. Robin flying to her nest with a bright piece of yellow cloth. "It is longer than she is, and now, with no shuttle or machinery, she is weaving it into the nest, tucking it into the grass that covers the mud bowl. Her home now looks like a party house and Cock Robin is pleased. He is dancing."

Tony thought the Mayor ought to know what the decoration meant and went to his back door to catch him before he came around his house and was accosted by Mary Alice.

"Sir," he said politely when the Mayor answered his knock, "a robin decorates her nest the day before she lays an egg. It takes her about four or five days to build her nest, one day to put in the lining of rootlets, and one day to decorate. Then, if it doesn't rain and soften the mud, she will lay the next day."

The Mayor was exceedingly interested and asked Tony how he knew this. He told him about his brother, Izzy, and the notes he had been taking for him. The Mayor stroked his chin and sized up Tony with his small brown eyes that were like drills. Under such scrutiny Tony felt self-conscious about his ears, which stuck out like cupboard doors, and the skin that was peeling off his sunburned nose. Just when he thought he was going to blush from embarrassment and disgrace himself, the Mayor stopped looking at him and slapped him across the shoulders in a friendly manner. He told him he certainly wanted to talk to him again.

"Perhaps very soon," he had said as he hurried toward the gate where Mary Alice and her two friends were waiting.

"Guess what?" Tony heard him say to the girls. "Tomorrow Cock Robin will be a proud papa."

The girls squealed and clapped. At the Commons they ran off to tell the news to three other girls and the Mayor dropped into the *Patent Reader* office.

The next morning, May 8, the paper carried a banner

headline about the blessed event. Tony read it on the porch, went to his room, picked up his field glasses, and was pleased to see an egg in the nest in the hat. He turned on his radio. The Mayor's voice was exuberant as he described the pretty egg and Cock Robin's singing commercial about it. Male robins never announce eggs, nor do females, but Tony forgave him the error. Then the Mayor cleared his throat. "Frank Lamberty of the Missatonic Mill," he said, "is celebrating this event in a particularly wonderful way. Today he will meet with the stockholders of the mill and discuss the purchasing of a tank truck to cart off the aniline dyes.

"And so, dear friends, Cock Robin's blue egg may mark the beginning of a new era—children catching fish, boys diving in the river, mothers and babies paddling their feet in the clear Missatonic while Cock Robins sing overhead. Thanks, Frank."

Tony turned off the radio and walked to his window. He winked at Cock Robin, picked up his books, and whistled all the way down the steps to the door.

As he opened it the Mayor was there to meet him. Before he could express his pleasure Mayor Joe asked in a worried voice why there was only one egg; he thought robins had five. Tony explained that songbirds lay one egg a day until their clutch is complete. "Four or five is a clutch for a robin," he said. "Then the female starts to incubate so that they all hatch at once." The Mayor seemed pleased with this information. He nodded and hurried across the street. Tony saw his square, beaver-shaped figure hustle around the corner drugstore. He reached the Commons just as Mayor Joe stepped into the office of the *Patent Reader*.

For the next four days the announcement of each egg was accompanied by photographs of the new sewage-disposal plant, the burial grounds of the DDT, and the maples and elms of Saddleboro "shimmering in the clean air."

When the fifth egg was laid the Mayor phoned Tony and asked him what came next. Tony said that the female would now brood the eggs and that this inter-lude was known as the "incubation period." He added that both birds would change their behavior during this time and started to tell the Mayor just how, but he had hung up.

"Cock Robin Hour" opened the next morning with the announcement by Mayor Joe that "Incubation Period has begun! Mrs. Robin is on her nest." He went on to say that "her feathers were spread and her head tilted up as she warmed her beautiful eggs.

"She just blinked," he said. "Now she is standing up and leaning down to . . . count her eggs. She is touch-ing each one and moving them. There are five," he said, then added, "five potential babies who will enjoy our clean and healthy town."

On the fifth day of incubation, Tony waited for the Mayor at his back door and suggested that perhaps Cock

Robin was not well. "Because," he said, "today you mentioned that he was sitting on the roof of your garden tool shed singing 'loud rock songs.' "

"You like that? I'm with this new generation of eighteen-year-old voters. Know all their terms."

"Well," Tony said, "the language is clever, but rarely does a male robin sit in the open and sing when his mate is incubating. He's very quiet so as not to attract predators. I hope he's all right."

The Mayor assured Tony that Cock Robin was fine. "He's got to be. He's got lots of worms in my yard and there's no DDT or carbon monoxide from cars in the air to harm him."

Tony walked behind the Mayor to his gate. Mary Alice and her friends were not there, and he took the opportunity to tell him that Mrs. Robin was not counting her eggs the other day, but turning them so that the embryos would not stick to the shells.

"Oh?" said Mayor Joe. "Well, a little colorful misinformation doesn't matter. It's the end results that count. That story got action. The high school kids are going to celebrate Incubation Period by cleaning out the underbrush in the Town Park on Saturday. And just before I left the house the Senior Citizens Club called and offered to paint the picnic tables and benches. Cock Robin's a boon to Saddleboro. Everyone's working for him. And that's what's important, not the details."

Nevertheless, the Mayor opened his program the next morning with a dramatic speech about Mrs. Robin turning her eggs as she displayed a wisdom far beyond man's. "Would you know enough to turn an egg to keep it from sticking to the shell?" he asked. "Our Cock Robin's wife does. So let's walk to church this Sunday to keep the air clean for her."

That afternoon Tony was on his way to the library when he heard his name shouted across the Commons and turned to see David Lowenthal beckoning him from the door of his office. Tony walked hesitantly past the fountain that sat in the center of the Commons and across the street to the office of the *Patent Reader*.

The editor was sitting at a desk piled high with papers. Nearby sat Sis Piekartz, an elderly spinster who had been a reporter for so many years before Lowenthal bought the paper that few could remember the days when she had not been at that desk. The president of the PTA, the mother of one of Mary Alice's friends, was dictating school news to her.

While waiting for the editor's attention Tony walked into the press room. Seever Jones, the printer, was setting type for the next edition. The odor of printer's ink filled the room. He went back to the office. Presently Editor Lowenthal glanced up from his work, seeing Tony at last.

"How long's this incubation period?" he asked without ceremony.

"Twelve to thirteen days," Tony replied promptly, "but since there was a frost the night before Mrs. Robin started incubating, I'd say thirteen for her."

"Thanks." He took out a calendar, counted the days, picked up the phone, and dialed.

"Joe!" he shouted. Tony wondered whether to remain or go. "Listen, that robin is going to sit on those eggs for another seven days. Then there'll be babies. Let's have a big rally and celebration, call it 'Cock Robin Day' and get everyone together for some speeches and fun!"

Tony could not hear what the Mayor said, but the editor grinned and said it was just a little idea he'd had to get the folks together in the Town Park for some propaganda about Saddleboro's victory over pollution. When he said the event might get statewide attention, the Mayor's voice vibrated the hardware in the telephone. Tony knew it was impolite to listen, but had no choice, and so he learned that a state committeeman named Bob Krampner was looking for a conservationist to fill the state senate seat "vacated by the sudden death of old Joe Sneider—may he rest in peace."

"I want that job!" The Mayor barked so loudly that Tony thought even Seever the printer could hear him. "Keep that robin on the front page."

Apparently Lowenthal was more interested in his idea about Cock Robin Day than the future of the Mayor.

"Yeah, yeah, Joe. Don't worry," he said. "Now, listen. Everyone will tote out of the picnic what he totes in. We'll have a big trash campaign, get everyone conscious of keeping the environment clean. I think Gordon at the drugstore will furnish tote bags. I'll print a little ad on them for him, free. Then I'll go down to the park when it's all over and write a story about how Saddleboro is leading the nation in cleaning up picnic grounds. Summer's coming, you know, and if I write it well the wire services might pick up the story and do us all some good. You get statewide publicity. I get ads . . . always do after a national story. And let's get a picture of that Cock Robin and his babies in your hat. Circulation has increased every time we've run a robin picture."

Lowenthal hung up, swung to his typewriter, and began to write. Tony hesitated, for he still did not know whether the editor wanted any more information from him. He was moving uncomfortably toward the door when the phone rang again and he heard Lowenthal say, "White birds? Thousands of them? Where? At Saddleboro Marsh? Thanks." He hung up.

"Seever," he shouted. "Got time to write a story?" When he answered "No" David told Sis to get out to the marsh. As she rose to leave she sighed in misery. Lowenthal groaned.

"Never mind," he said, "I'll do it from here. This is my kind of story—white birds, clean air." He pulled out the paper on which he had been typing, spun in a new sheet, and began to write. Suddenly he looked up at Tony. "What can I do for you?" he asked. "Oh!" He smiled. "Excuse me. Thanks for the information. That'll be all."

Tony walked home from school by way of the Saddleboro Marsh and saw that the birds were herring gulls. He wondered why they were there and crept to the edge of the water. When one stabbed a dead fish he saw that hundreds of bass and sunfish were floating on the water. This both perplexed and worried him. He walked slowly through the meadow and climbed over the stone fence onto Elm Street.

The next morning Tony listened to the "Cock Robin Hour" while he dressed. When the Mayor described a "jazzy Cock Robin" he dashed downstairs to get the paper. His father was reading it as he drank his coffee.

"Let me have the weather page, please," Tony said urgently. His father passed it across the table.

Tony was glad to see that the high pressure area that had hung over New England for the past three weeks showed no signs of changing from sunshine to rain. That would be disastrous, for the Mayor had said Cock Robin was "sitting on his tool shed all puffed up and looking like a proud papa." To Tony that meant he was sick. A cold rain might take his life before the picnic on May 25. He phoned the Mayor's house to warn him, but he had left for a meeting with Committeeman Krampner and would not be back until late.

The next morning Tony read Lowenthal's story about the gulls. It was a fine piece of literature about birds flocking to beautiful Saddleboro, but no mention was made of the fact that they were herring gulls who were eating dead fish. Under the story was a boxed announcement that Mayor and Mrs. Dambrowski would serve fresh lemonade—not bottles, no cans, no artificial flavoring—to all the kids who came to the park after school to pick up and prepare for Cock Robin Day. That sounded good to Tony.

Late that afternoon he got his lemonade and was carrying it across the baseball diamond when he noticed that the ground was covered with anthills. He collected several ants in his empty cup and hurried home to look them up in his insect book. They were yellow ants that almost never appeared in vast numbers unless there were no insect predators like spiders or birds to control them. In other words, they represented a missing link in the food cycle. He mentioned this to the Mayor the next morning.

"Lots of ants?" Mayor Joe said. "Hmmm. They might spoil the picnic."

"They mean something is wrong with the ecology of the park."

"Well, we can't have it both ways. We've banned DDT, and that's right. I talked to a chemist before I issued the ordinance. He said DDT was a hydrocarbon. It takes it two hundred thousand years, or a geological age, to break down into safe elements. Because it is hard to destroy, it gets passed from plant to worm to fish, chicken, and man. We'll have to put up with the ants."

"I didn't mean we should spray them with DDT," Tony said. "I meant that Saddleboro is not as clean an environment as we think. There must be something else wrong to have so many ants . . . like trillions of them."

"Now, Tony," the Mayor said. "The air-pollution count has been zero in Saddleboro for weeks. I don't think you have to worry."

Despite his seeming confidence, Mayor Joe called Tony that evening and asked him if he knew any safe pesticides.

"Yes, pyrethrum, rotenone, serin. Do you mind if I ask why?"

"Dave Lowenthal and I went down to the park at noon yesterday and there *are* quite a few ants around. Just thought we might have John Pierce at the hardware store bring down some safe sprays in case the ants offend the ladies. Dave will announce it in the paper and write a story about the good insecticides."

"Oh," replied Tony. "I'll give him some of my brother's notes on biological controls, like parasites that kill beetles. They're even better."

On the eleventh day of incubation Mayor Joe sounded somewhat concerned as he spoke on the air.

"Mamma's off the nest," he said. "She's been gone since six A.M." He went on to say that according to his wife, Ellen, who had been keeping tabs, Mrs. Robin never stayed away from her eggs longer than ten to fifteen minutes. He also added that Ellen had seen Cock Robin call Mrs. Robin from her eggs when she needed to eat. She had dined until Cock Robin had felt it was time for her to return. He had then sung a song that sent her home.

"Maybe this morning Cock Robin forgot to scold the old lady," he had said and chuckled.

"I'll stick around the house this morning and let you know when she comes back." The Mayor went off the air, and an ad for John Pierce's nontoxic insecticides came on.

At five minutes to eight, much to the relief of almost every listener, Mayor Joe announced that Mrs. Robin was back on her eggs. He then hopped in his car and was driving toward the Town Hall when Tony dashed around his house to warn him that the robins were not well.

The next day Mayor Joe came on the air and said of Cock Robin simply, "He looks mighty proud." He spent the remainder of his radio time complimenting the parents of Saddleboro on the excellent job their children had done at the Town Park.

"It's neat as a pin. I was down there yesterday and couldn't even find a leaf or weed, much less a gum wrapper. You've taught your children well."

He also complimented the ladies of the Garden Club for their plantings around the park entrance. He had a few minutes left and spent it describing his bright green lawn and his beautiful flowers that were sparkling in the clean air of Saddleboro.

The Mayor's lawn was not only the most beautiful in town, but had become famous during his campaign, for he had talked about it constantly, telling how he had used a certain nitrogen-rich fertilizer to produce the emerald color. Furthermore, he had gotten the votes of the Garden Club when he had given them his secret formula at a membership meeting one night.

When Tony left for school the Mayor was again at his door.

"I'm really concerned about Cock Robin," he said. "He's been sitting on the tool-shed roof all morning. He hasn't flown once, just twitches. What does that mean?"

Tony told the Mayor to wait, crossed the street, and walked slowly into his yard. He came back shaking his head.

"He doesn't look good," he said. "When a bird fluffs up as much as that, he's sick. Maybe you shouldn't talk about him until we find out what's wrong . . . just talk about Mrs. Robin."

The Mayor, however, announced the following morning that Cock Robin was leaping from the shed roof to the ground in great excitement, "like a father pacing the floor of the hospital."

"See you the day after tomorrow," he sang out. "Saddleboro will have five beautiful baby robins to cheer about."

Tony ran out of his house, sped to the Mayor's back door, and boldly knocked. When the Mayor appeared he told him that Cock Robin was not pacing like a father in a hospital at all, but was so poorly coordinated he was flopping. "He's sick, and he's trying to get away from the marsh hawk," he said, pointing to a large broad-winged bird above the Mayor's house.

"The marsh hawk?"

"Yes, he's been circling your house since dawn."

"I'll shoot him!" he exclaimed.

"Don't do that. He's important to the ecology, too. He takes the sick animals and leaves the well ones."

"Then I'll tell Sam, my gardener, to stay out in that yard all day and keep that hawk away. Cock Robin's got to live! A newspaper man from the capital is coming to take Bob Krampner's picture with him. Bob Krampner likes that bird and Bob Krampner's important to my future!

"SAM!" the Mayor shouted. The stoop-shouldered gardener appeared, promised he would scare off the hawk, asked which fertilizer he wanted to use on the far corner of the lawn where the grass was bleaching, and carried a box of Japanese beetle dust to the rose garden. The Mayor and Tony walked to the gate. Tony was about to tell him about the robin's food problems when Mary Alice dashed around the house.

"How are the Cock Robins?" she asked, pushing her bangs out of her eyes.

"Fine, fine. The little mother is getting used to me," the Mayor said proudly. "She cocks her eye when I peek out the curtain and chirps softly. She's a dear. Now you run along, Mary Alice; I must talk to Tony. He's my robin aide. Get all my information from him."

Who Really Killed Cock Robin?

Mary Alice gave Tony a cold look and walked off haughtily.

Tony grinned. This was the first time she had not been able to overwhelm him and usurp the Mayor's attention. He was grateful to Cock Robin and Izzy for that. He was becoming an expert on robins. As Mary Alice's heels clicked down the street with less zip and confidence, Tony sucked air deep into his lungs and felt his shoulders go back. Turning to the Mayor, he told him that robins do not feed their hatchlings earthworms but the green larvae of the cabbage looper. These, he added, are terribly scarce. He had not seen one all spring. "I'm worried about the food supply. I still think those trillions of ants mean that some animal is missing from the food chain for some mysterious reason."

The Mayor put his hand on Tony's shoulder and assured him that his yard was a robin's gourmet restaurant and that all would be fine on the dawn of Cock Robin Day.

"By the way, and this is between you and me, I haven't heard the spring frogs this year. Are they okay?"

"Well," Tony hesitated. "Come here." He led the Mayor to the roadside where neatly drained ditches led off down the hill. "When you banned DDT, the ladies of the Garden Club came out and drained these ditches so there wouldn't be any mosquitoes. That's why there aren't any frogs on Elm Street, but I did hear them in the marsh until about April eighteenth." The Mayor was listening attentively and Tony continued.

"My brother, Izzy, told me to note all the sounds I heard. Last night, while looking over my notes, I was surprised to see I had not mentioned frogs after mid-April. I thought I had just forgotten, but I guess not. The truth is there are no frogs."

"What do you make of it? I love those harbingers of spring."

"I still think something's wrong in Saddleboro," Tony said, "but I don't know enough to know what it is. What you've done so far is right. Izzy said so before he left. But . . ." John Pierce came down the street and interrupted Tony to tell the Mayor something about Ward Three, the large voting area in which he lived. The Mayor stopped to talk about it and Tony walked slowly on to school.

At nine minutes past six the following morning the phone rang in the kitchen of 65 Elm Street and Tony Isidoro got the word from Mary Alice that Cock Robin was dead. He sprinted to his bedroom window, picked up his field glasses, saw the robin was dead, and noted the details.

Walking slowly into Izzy's room, he stared at the pile of ecology maps, then thumbed through Izzy's notes. The telephone rang for a second time. He ran downstairs and as Mary Alice had predicted, it was Mayor Joe.

"Tony, Cock Robin is dead! Find out who killed him! This is very embarrassing."

"Embarrassing, sir?"

"I've no one to accuse. Lamberty's mill has not been dumping dyes since long before the first egg was laid."

2. The Case of the Detergents

Tony put down the telephone and thoughtfully climbed the stairs. He wandered back to Izzy's room and sat down before the maps of Saddleboro again. He felt confused as he thumbed through them. Why, he wondered, had Izzy drawn in all the watersheds and wind directions? He had even recorded the altitude of hills and valleys. When he came to a map of the rocks and soils under Saddleboro, he was lost in the field of ecology. What did all this have to do with robins? He got up, paced the room, then flipped aimlessly through Izzy's card file. He found a note that said five baby robins had hatched in the Isidoros' apple tree on May 23 two years ago. At the bottom was this entry: "Bachelor male took over apple-tree female after her mate disappeared, possibly to Korkner's cat."

Tony grinned. He was pleased to learn baby robins could have a stepfather. He was reading how the new male fed the youngsters twenty times a day when Mr. Isidoro went down the back steps to the kitchen and turned on the radio.

"Tone!" he called. "Where are you? Cock Robin is dead! The Mayor's speaking."

"Yeah, Pop, I know," Tony said as he came down the steps slowly. He swung his leg over the back of his chair, and sat down. "The Mayor just called me."

The Mayor was interviewing David Lowenthal. He called him an expert on conservation, "the man who brought the *Patent Reader* to inform people about ecology."

"Dave," the Mayor said, "who really did kill Cock Robin?"

"Detergents killed him, Joe," Dave answered conclusively. "I have a report here from the Kansas State Geological Survey. It says that pre-soaks and most detergents have arsenic in them now. This scientist found fifty-nine thousand parts per billion of arsenic in several of these products. Ten parts per billion in drinking water is the limit the U.S. Public Health Service will tolerate. He also found this deadly poison in alarming amounts in the Kansas River."

"How would that kill the bird? He nested on my porch."

"Of all our songbirds, the robin loves water best. Loves to splash in it, bathe, drink. Our Cock Robin, true to his breed, obviously sloshed in the Missatonic and died. Even his feathers were affected, as you said yourself on the 'Cock Robin Hour.' They were frumpy and puffed. Detergents take the oil off the feathers of ducks; the ducks sink and drown. They obviously took the oil off the feathers of Cock Robin; he grew cold at night, lost weight, the arsenic took effect, and he died."

"But what about the sewage-disposal plant? Doesn't it take the arsenic and detergents out?"

"Not all of them. You know that, Joe. No sewage-disposal plant is one hundred percent efficient. And it doesn't take much detergent to kill a little bird. Furthermore, the farmers upstream are not connected to the plant and they all use detergents to clean their milk cans and machines. Their drainpipes empty into the Missatonic."

"It's indeed a sad day," said the Mayor. "Our beautiful robin is dead. But we have all learned a lesson. Don't use detergents. Not only do they bubble up and congest the singing Missatonic, but also kill birds and fish. In our grocery store, you'll find soaps you can use instead, and many housewives in this area know how to make soap from fat and lye. Get in touch with your neighbor. See if she can help you to keep the birds of Saddleboro singing.

"Do not be discouraged. Tomorrow Cock Robin's babies will hatch and we will celebrate Cock Robin Day as wiser and more informed environmentalists. Good day and Good Soap Using."

Tony turned off the radio.

"Detergents didn't kill him," he shouted at the radio. "That's nonsense!"

"Maybe he wants to take a crack at the farmers," Tony's father said. "He didn't get their votes."

Tony scarcely heard this. He was furious. The Mayor had asked him to find out who killed Cock Robin and then had solved it in one interview with David Lowenthal. The editor was no scientist. How could he know it was detergents without testing the bird and the river? He was only guessing.

Tony slumped on the kitchen table and ran his hand through his hair.

What could he do now? He was the Mayor's nature detective with no case. He chuckled at his ridiculous position, decided to forget the whole thing, and got out the math homework he had not finished.

As he opened the book the words of David Lowenthal rang in his head. The more he thought about them, the more he wanted to find out what really killed the bird. He closed his book, planted his elbows on the table, his chin in his fists, and made up his mind to continue with the job he had been assigned—to find out who *really* killed Cock Robin. He wanted to know.

He grinned with satisfaction only to realize he did not know how to begin an investigation. After pacing the room he decided the first thing to do was prove whether or not detergents *had* killed Cock Robin. Again he asked himself, "How?" Then he remembered seeing a kit in Izzy's room and dashed upstairs to look at it again.

Just as he hoped, it was a water-testing kit, a simple device developed for the U.S. Army to check on the safety of drinking water. The "laboratory" was a box of plastic cards, each of which reacted to one or more chemical pollutants. When dipped in a river or stream, a card would change color if a specific chemical or hard metal were present. The color could be checked against a chart to determine the amounts present—none, sublethal, lethal. He flipped through the cards: nitrogen, lead, sulphur dioxide. Finally he found one for phosphates, one of the pollutants in detergents. He put the kit and his notebook into a small knapsack, shook his fist at the Mayor's house, and went down the front steps and out the door. Mary Alice, long legs flying, was running toward the Mayor's gate. Tony waved to her and crossed the street.

"Funeral! Funeral!" she exclaimed. "We're going to have a funeral at eleven o'clock recess. Be sure to come." He grinned, and as he stepped up on the sidewalk beside her, realized for the first time that he towered over her by at least six inches. She was little, all right, but like an aggressive bird, could puff up to appear bigger.

"The Mayor's furious!" Mary Alice's eyes twinkled. "He thinks a funeral is bad publicity. But Mrs. Dambrowski and I think it will be lovely. We're going to make it nice—lots of spring flowers and all. I'm writing a conservation prayer."

"Mary Alice," Tony said, "I'm the Mayor's detective on what is now the Cock Robin Murder Case, and what I need to know is when your Dad last dumped dyes in the river."

"Detergents did it," she snapped. "They must have. The mill only dumps dyes once every two or three months; *and*, Mr. Detective, the last time was March eleventh."

"Thanks."

Mary Alice unlatched the gate as Mrs. Dambrowski stepped out the door.

"Sam!" the Mayor's wife called to the gardener. "Will you get those lilies and daffodils over to the fountain in the Commons right away? And, oh, Sam, make the hole nice and neat, please." She saw Mary Alice. "You'd better come in the back door. Mrs. Robin is a little nervous this morning."

As Tony jumped over the stone wall into the meadow that bordered the marsh, he saw Mayor Joe come down his back steps. The man paused, then walked quickly across his lawn. He picked up Cock Robin and stared at him. Tony wondered what he was thinking. He had probably never held a bird before. Was he admiring his beautiful feathers, the intricate scales on his legs and feet, the perfection of his wings? No, Tony thought, he was probably cursing him for dying before the Cock Robin Day picnic.

The Mayor walked back to his house and Tony went on toward the river, glancing thoughtfully at the Saddleboro Marsh as he hurried along. Once a sharp bend or oxbow in the river, it had been cut off when the Missatonic changed its course hundreds of years ago. Gradually the oxbow had filled in and reeds had appeared along its edges, until it was now a freshwater marsh, one of the most interesting in the state, according to Izzy. Once Saddleboro Marsh had been considered for a town dump, because it was "useless" land, but the Hunting Club had complained so vigorously that the mayor at that time was forced to purchase land farther down the river for refuse.

As Tony strode along he could see the reeds and rushes undulating in the wind like waves on the ocean. Insects flitted above the plants and the sun sparkled on the water. The marsh was beautiful. He hurried through the red-maple grove which Mayor Joe's Administration had bought and given to the park. It bordered the Mayor's yard and garden and, as everyone knew, enhanced his property. Few people cared, however, for the Town Park was the pride of Saddleboro. The entire woodland of ancient beeches and maples looked down on the rolling river and cloistered camping, picnicking, and play areas that were enjoyed by the people of Saddleboro. Tony's father went there almost every evening in the summer to play the Italian game of boccie with his friends from the old country and watch the Polish people who came to the park to play accordions and dance.

Tony walked to the river, removed his shoes, rolled

up his blue jeans, and waded into a shallow spot. He pulled an adhesive cover off the plastic card labeled "arsenic" and dipped it into the water. Nothing happened. He flipped through the kit, took out the card for the phosphates in detergents, and held that in the water. Slowly it turned a faint pink. He compared it with the chart and found there was less than one-hundredth part per billion of this chemical in the water, far below the color labeled "sublethal." He tested for nitrogen and found this count high. Then he dipped in a chlorinated hydrocarbon card, which would indicate the presence of DDT if it turned blue. Pulling it slowly out of the water, he frowned, put it back in, took it out, and scratched his head. It was green, not blue. He wondered what *that* meant.

Wading ashore, he walked home through the marsh listening for frogs and looking for their eggs. When the school bell rang he darted across the meadow and through town to the public school on Pine Street.

He was late, but his teacher seemed not to care. She was shouting to the kids to sit down and get to work.

"The funeral is not until eleven o'clock," she fairly screamed. "And we have three pages of math to cover before we can go!" Tony opened his book but did no work. He was watching the clock.

At eleven he slipped out of the back door of his classroom and darted across the playground to the shortcut that led to the Commons. He wanted to catch Mayor Joe before he spoke about detergents. He was too late;

the Mayor and his wife were already at the fountain. Mrs. Dambrowski was telling Sam where to place a huge armload of flowers from the yards of the citizens of Saddleboro.

The Commons looked peaceful, but Mayor Joe did not. He was pacing before the little grave with a scowl on his face. Mary Alice was right, he did not want this funeral. When the schoolchildren filed down Pine and called to him, however, he forced a smile, waved, and stepped into the group of business people.

Tony sat down under an elm across from the *Patent Reader* and watched the kids romp over the grass, shouting and laughing. The door of the newspaper office opened. David Lowenthal and Seever Jones came out carrying a large brass bell. They struggled to the fountain and put it down. "What's that for?" Mayor Joe barked.

"To toll," answered Lowenthal mournfully. He stood up and rubbed his arms. "It's off my old World War II destroyer. I got it when they made razor blades out of my ship." He ran his fingers through his graying hair. Mayor Joe stared icily at him and Tony chuckled; the funeral was going to be nice, after all. He got up and moved to a spot where he could see Mrs. Dambrowski. She was holding a shoe box decorated with flowers— Cock Robin's casket. As she stepped forward Mayor Joe wedged himself behind John Pierce and David Lowenthal. But for the checkered sleeve of his jacket, he was obscured from view.

A breeze stirred and Mary Alice swished past Tony. She walked swiftly around him and stood beside Mrs. Dambrowski, as down Hardscrabble, over the grounds of the library, and across the Commons came five high school boys carrying a large package.

"They shouldn't be here," somebody said. "This is for the little kids." But nobody sent them away.

Mary Alice, dressed in the tailored uniform of the parochial school, stepped forward and raised her hand.

"Please be silent!" she shouted. The children giggled, moved closer to her, then quieted down, and Mary Alice had the podium.

"Dear friends," she began. "This is indeed a moment of sorrow for Saddleboro. Our beloved Cock Robin is dead. He was a beautiful bird, full of life and vitality. He sang to his mate at dawn, dined with her on the lawn, and defended her against hawk and cat. He could not, however, defend himself against man.

"Man pollutes the air with automobile exhaust and noxious insecticides. He pollutes rippling rivers with detergents so that his clothes might be clean, and in so doing kills animals that share this earth with us. Today, in memory of Cock Robin, we will all resolve never to use detergents again. We children can help. Wash your face with soap.

"To replace laundry detergents, add to a box of soap powder half a large box of washing soda and mix them together in a big bag. Remove the box of detergent from your mother's laundry room and put the bag in its place.

Also, use a bar of plain soap when you do the dishes. You'll be surprised how clean it will get them.

"Since our parents could not keep Cock Robin alive, we kids will devote ourselves to keeping his babies alive. Tomorrow they will hatch and Cock Robin will live again in them if we throw out our detergents and use soap to keep our waterways sparkling. How many will do this?"

"I, I, I," shouted the children as they raised their hands and looked around to see who had not. One of the Pierce twins had his hands in his pocket. His sister nudged him, grabbed his arm, and raised it. Cheers went up.

"I've been asked by my father," Mary Alice shouted above the din, "to announce the new policy of the Missatonic Mill. Today, a new truck will carry the aniline dyes that have polluted our river for much too long from the mill to the dump. It's a birthday present to the baby robins."

The children clapped, the Mayor peered around David Lowenthal, looking first surprised, then pleased, and raised his fingers in the victory sign.

Tony was fascinated by the whole funeral and was staring at Mary Alice, wondering how she had managed the truck, when he heard someone say it was her birthday and that her daddy always gave her what she wanted.

As Tony thought about that, Mary Alice's chin lowered, she took the shoe box from Mrs. Dambrowski, walked the five steps to the grave, and put the box in the ground.

"Aw-w," murmured the children. Sam covered the box quickly and Mrs. Dambrowski laid a chain of bluebells on the grave.

"Let's all sing 'America the Beautiful,'" she said, lifted her hand, and directed the chorus.

"Amen," shouted Mary Alice when the song was done. The funeral appeared to be over but it was not. The five high school boys had inflated a huge war-surplus balloon with helium and it was rising behind the Mayor's head. On it were printed the words: WHO REALLY KILLED COCK ROBIN? Under these words was a list of names that Tony barely had time to read before the balloon sailed across the grave, the children's heads, and the tall trees of Town Park. He did, however, have time to see Mayor Joe's and Frank Lamberty's names. Mary Alice apparently saw too, for she turned very red and moved closer to Mrs. Dambrowski.

"Mayor Joe!" one of the five high school boys shouted. "Speech! Speech!" Mayor Joe ignored him. He shouted again, the young kids chimed in, and Lowenthal whispered something in Mayor Joe's ear. The Mayor nodded and raised his hand. When the funeral goers were silent, he stepped forward.

"We will have a ten-minute toll for Cock Robin," he announced. "Every child may toll the bell once. Let us keep Saddleboro clean for Cock Robin's babies!" He leaned down, grabbed the bell strap, and let it go. A deep clang rang out. He then handed the strap to a little boy who tolled not once but three times. From that moment on there was no opportunity for the Mayor to speak. The children were screaming and fighting for the bell strap. Mayor Joe slipped around David Lowenthal and hurried across the green toward Town Hall.

Tony caught up with him at the steps.

"Sir," he said. Mayor Joe looked around.

"Sorry, Tony, I'm busy."

"But, Mayor Joe, it was *not* detergents. Look." He pulled out his water-testing kit.

The Mayor went on up the steps. Tony ran after him.

"You asked me to find out who killed Cock Robin and I'm going to." The Mayor hesitated but did. not stop walking.

"Can we have an autopsy?" Tony called.

The Mayor spun around and halted abruptly. "NO!"

"Well, I've tested the river and there are practically no detergents in it. But there are other things that might have caused his death."

The Mayor's hand slipped around Tony's shoulder in a patronizing manner.

"Let's let well enough alone, Tone," he said. "We'll have the cute little babies to talk about tomorrow. After all, birds do die."

"Yes, that's true," Tony said. "And others replace them. You'll probably have a new male in the morning."

The Mayor's hand fell from Tony's shoulder.

"What?"

"Sure. When a male dies or is killed, a bachelor male usually takes over his mate and land almost immediately."

"Tony, you mean I didn't have to announce that Cock Robin is dead!"

"Well, yes, you *had* to announce it. He *did* die."

Mayor Joe's shoulders slumped as he asked Tony to tell him more about foster bird parents.

"That's very interesting," he said when Tony had told him about Izzy's notes on the robin in his yard. "Now let's forget Cock Robin."

"But, sir, this may concern more than just robins. What about the frogs? You yourself said they weren't singing. And they aren't. There are barely any in the marsh."

With that he had the Mayor's full attention and so took the opportunity to show him the chemical cards.

"This is a test taken in the Missatonic. It's for detergents. See, they're almost nil. But look at this one." He handed the Mayor the green card marked "chlorinated hydrocarbon." "This is for man-made chemicals like DDT. But it's not DDT," he explained, "because that would turn the paper blue. I think I should investigate. The paper's awful dark. There's a lot of whatever it is in the river."

"Okay, Tony, investigate. But no autopsy. Understand?"

Tony shrugged his shoulders, mumbled "I'm an investigator," and jumped down the steps. The bell was tolling erratically as the children heckled it with sticks. They were dragged away by a teacher as another herded those who had had their turn back toward the school. Tony followed them.

As he slipped into his desk chair the bell stopped ringing and Saddleboro was quiet again.

The half-moon was low in a clear sky when Tony climbed out his bedroom window, tiptoed across his porch roof, and slid down the rainspout to the ground. Taking a familiar route through back yards, he passed the newspaper office as the Town Hall clock struck two. The street lamps and a night light on the front of the drugstore illuminated the deserted Commons. Tony darted across the street just as the Saddleboro police car came around the corner on its rounds. He ducked behind the statue of Cotton Mather, an early New England clergyman and writer. The car stopped at the intersection while Sergeant Sears glanced up and down the streets, accelerated the engine, and headed toward the newer section of town. Tony darted to the fountain.

In the semi-darkness he carefully dug up the casket,

opened it, and stuffed Cock Robin into his shirt. He replaced the box and earth, and put the bluebells back, and dashed away. He came out on Elm Street two doors from the Mayor's house.

After climbing the rainspout and crawling back through his window, he got into his pajamas and walked down the steps to the kitchen. He wrapped Cock Robin in waxed paper and put him in the refrigerator.

"That you, Tony?" his all-hearing mother called out.

"Yeah, I'm getting a glass of milk." And he did.

3. The Deepening Disaster

The morning air on Cock Robin Day was so dry that the new leaves on Tony's apple tree were beginning to droop when he got out of bed and focused his field glasses on the nest in the Mayor's hat. Mrs. Robin was sitting on it. No restless behavior told him that her eggs were breaking open. He went back to bed. At six-thirty he checked her once more and saw the Mayor peek through his curtain as a male robin flew up from the ground. The bird sat quietly in the top of the hickory tree. Tony set his alarm for seven, turned his radio on low, and dozed until the "Cock Robin Hour."

"Good morning, Saddleboro." Tony turned up the volume. "What a beautiful day to celebrate. My lawn is emerald green, yellow daffodils frame it, and the air is clear and sweet. Mrs. Robin is sitting on her nest so I can't see the babies."

He then talked about the picnic, the fun everyone would have, and how good it was of the drugstore owner, Hank Gordon, to donate the tote-in–tote-out bags.

When the political commercials were over Mayor Joe bellowed out the news that Mrs. Robin had a new husband to help her raise her brood. Tony was not so sure. The male had not yet sung, something he must do if he were going to remain, but the Mayor was ignorant of this fact and therefore confident.

"He has taken our beloved Cock Robin's place and will help Mrs. Robin bring Saddleboro's baby robins into the clear air."

Next Mayor Joe talked about his lawn. He proudly told of a "natural powder" he had bought at the hardware store that killed ugly fungi and made brown grass green again. After recommending it, he ended the program by saying that since it was still too early to know if the babies had hatched, he would go off the air until he was an eyewitness to the blessed event. "Keep tuned to our station."

When Tony came downstairs his mother was speculating about what the Mayor would do if the babies didn't hatch today.

"I'm guessing they won't," she said, "and he has no alternative lined up."

"You may be right," Tony answered.

The Deepening Disaster

At eight o'clock he heard the new male sing from the hickory tree and ran upstairs to look at Mrs. Robin again. She was still broody. Nothing could be hatching under a bird that sat in such a deep trance. He sat down on his bed and thought over the data.

Cock Robin was dead, his babies still unhatched, no frogs were singing, the cabbage-looper worms were scarce, there were too many ants, and the fish were dying. As he added up all this he suddenly realized that Cock Robin was not just a dead bird in someone's yard, he was part of something bigger—a town, perhaps a county, even a whole state.

Izzy's stacks of wind, soil, marsh, and industrial maps came to mind. He had compiled them for some reason. What were those maps telling him? How many mysteries did he really have to solve? He decided he had better find out and find out quickly.

Rushing to the refrigerator, he opened the door, put Cock Robin in his shirt, and hurried to the garage for his bike.

Swiftly he pedaled past the Commons, wove in and out of the high school band members who had gathered on Pine Street to practice tunes for the picnic, and took the highway to the campus of the State College.

Parking his bike next to the Zoology Building, he leaped up the steps three at a time, paused on the second floor, turned to the right, and hurried down the corridor to the histochemical laboratory.

Tony had been to this lab with Izzy and knew that

43.

histochemistry was not just chemistry, but the science of what chemicals do to animal tissues like muscle, bone, and nerves. He had learned this from Izzy's friend, Rob Cunningham, who was also a graduate student. He had once lived down the street from the Isidoros and had wandered the hills and river bank with Izzy when they were boys. When Rob's parents moved away, he had taken up residence at the college, where he was getting his doctoral degree in histochemistry. One day while Tony was visiting the lab, Rob had looked at the tissues of a bass under a microscope and told him that the fish had died of dioxin poison, one of the chemicals in weed killers. Tony had been very impressed and now hoped Rob could do the same for Cock Robin.

As he opened the door, Rob looked up from his microscope.

"Tony!" He grinned and jumped to his feet.

Rob looked different, Tony thought, then realized he had grown an Abe Lincoln beard.

"What're you doing here?" he asked.

Tony took the package out of his shirt, opened it, and placed the dead robin on the lab table.

"Would you do me a favor and perform an autopsy on this bird. I'd like to know what killed him."

Rob turned the bird over, then looked at Tony.

"This couldn't be the Cock Robin of Saddleboro, by any chance?"

Tony grinned sheepishly.

"Grave robbin', eh?"

Tony laughed at the pun and nodded.

"I'll do it," Rob said. "In fact, I'd be delighted to. I've been following his story." He reached across the table and turned up his transistor radio. Music was playing. "I'm dialed in on the Mayor, now. Have been for days. What's all this nonsense about detergents?"

"He's convinced himself it's true. But I tested the Missatonic with Izzy's water-pollution kit. There's no arsenic in it, and very little phosphate from detergents. However, something *is* in that water."

He took his notebook out of his hip pocket, opened it, and handed Rob the green card. "This is a test for DDT. But it's the wrong color. Should be blue."

"Hmm." Rob studied it, asked Tony a few questions, made notes, looked them over, and shrugged. "I'm baffled. Got any dope on the white birds?" When Tony told him that they were herring gulls who were eating dead fish, he suggested that he and Tony meet soon to study the marsh.

"Something's off balance around here," he said as he put down his pencil and pulled at his beard. "About one week after the Mayor started his program," Rob was looking at the notes he had jotted down during the Mayor's radio program, "he was describing a bird suffering from some chemical poisoning. Cock Robin fluffed, fluttered, and shook. That was no proud papa act. He was dying." He turned toward the telephone. "I'm going to give my chemist friend, Craig, a call. He's got some gear on the roof of the building that picks up pollutants in the air like radioactive particles, lead, DDT, and sulphur dioxide, stuff that comes from burning coal and oil. Let's see if he's got any dope that will help. What day did Cock Robin arrive?"

"April twenty-ninth. But the frogs stopped singing about April eighteenth."

Rob dialed, but there was no answer at the chemistry lab. He picked up Cock Robin, took him to the microtome, a tissue-cutting instrument, and said he was going to look at the fatty tissues in the muscles. He explained that if the fat cells around the nerves were destroyed he would know the bird had died of DDT poisoning. If not, he would make slides of the bone tissues and internal organs to determine what other chemicals were present.

"Hard metals like lead, mercury, strontium, and titanium are turning up in the bodies of dead birds and fish," he said.

"Where are they coming from?"

"The lead is coming from lead pipes in old houses and rain wash from streets where automobile exhaust settles. There's lead in gasoline exhaust, you know. It washes into rivers through storm sewers and comes to rest in rivers, pools, and bays. The mercury, on the other hand, is getting into plants and animals by way of caustic soda, a mercury-filled product used in industrial centers. My friend Craig told me all this. He's an expert on hard metals. I specialize in the chlorinated hydrocarbons like DDT, DDE, DDD, dieldrin heptachlor: the pesticides."

Rob took his dissecting instruments out of a drawer and bent over Cock Robin.

"I'll call you as soon as I know anything," he said. "Meanwhile, try to find where that green reaction is coming from. It *is* strange. Test upriver, down, in the marsh, around the Mayor's yard."

He asked Tony to leave the green card for Craig and the head of the department, Dr. Melvin. Then he told him he could pick up more cards at the supply department in the basement and set to work.

As Tony approached the town he heard a rumble and looked up to see a storm forming over the mountains. He wondered if it was going to rain and spoil the picnic.

At Pine Street he decided to test the river again and biked down Maple to the park in time to help John Pierce lift three cartons of nontoxic spray from the back of the station wagon. They put them under a tree.

"Hope his stuff sells," John said to Tony. "That David Lowenthal has been telling everyone it kills bugs slower than DDT. Doesn't exactly boost sales."

"Why don't you sell repellents, the stuff you put on yourself to keep off flies and mosquitoes?" Tony asked. "You don't need to spray. Repellents would keep the ants off people and wouldn't kill good insects."

John Pierce glanced at him and said he would bring a carton of repellents to the picnic.

Who Really Killed Cock Robin?

Tony walked toward the river, pausing on the way to watch an electrician from the mill set up a microphone. The five high school boys who had let the balloon go at the funeral came up to the bandstand and tacked up a poster: DID *you* KILL COCK ROBIN?

Tony thought about that. He went to the river and dipped the card, and once more it turned green. Then he became confused. Some duckweed, tiny floating circles of plant life that only grow in clean water, grew where he had tested. If the water was clean, and it must be if the duckweed was growing, why then, did the paper react to a chemical? Suddenly he thought of an answer. The sewage-disposal plant was above him. He knew that it treated the water with certain harmless chemicals before dumping it into the river. One of these must have turned the paper green instead of blue. The mysterious chemical, he convinced himself, was not harmful after all. He thought for a moment. If this were true, then the water above the plant should not color the card.

Jumping to his feet, he ran past the baseball field on his way to his bike. A low moan arose from the diamond. He stopped and looked around. The entire field was humming with bees. Why bees? He walked toward the pitcher's box, realizing gradually that the ants had created a new ecosystem, small but fascinating. They had carried up grains of sand from the earth as they made their underground tunnels and piled them on the surface. In the sand, bluettes, flowers that love poor soil, had taken root, grown, and bloomed. The bees had come to the flowers for nectar and pollen. But that was not the end of the story. Tony got down on his hands and knees and watched an ant carry a dead bee down a hole. Bees only live about thirty days, he had heard somewhere, and they often die at work. When they fell, the ants picked them up and took them down in their tunnels to feed to their young or larvae. Tony watched the tiny world go around as ant dug sand, sand grew plant, plant attracted bee, and bee was harvested by the ant.

Now he wondered what would happen when the picnickers came to the park. They would probably get stung and spray the bees with the nontoxic chemicals Mr. Pierce would be selling. The thousands of dead bees would provide more food for the ants. They would lay more eggs, feed more babies. The babies would mature and make more hills. The hills would grow more flowers and the flowers would attract more bees.

He could see a plague upon the park unless he found out why there were so many ants in the first place. He stood up and looked around. The sky was bright and clear, but for the thunderhead over the mountain. He glanced along the river edge and saw that other eddies were bright with duckweed. He smelled the breeze from the woods. It was fresh and good. He shrugged and decided to clear up one matter before he took on another.

Picking up his bike, he pedaled up Maple headed for

Pine Street and Crow Hill Road, planning to test the water above the plant. As he reached Pine, he saw a crowd of people milling excitedly in front of the drugstore. Members of the band jumped and waved their instruments, and a boy was climbing Cotton Mather's statue. The high school cheerleaders were turning cartwheels. The baby robins, he knew, had hatched.

"There are two. There are two of them!" Tony heard Mary Alice shout to her friend, Ginger Pierce. He wove through the cheerleaders and braked his bike beside her. She smiled at him and put her finger over her lips. "Sssh."

"Two babies!" the Mayor said over the blasting drugstore radio. "This is, indeed, a day to celebrate! I wish everyone could see them. They are tiny, but already look too big to have come out of those little shells. They have big red mouths, rimmed with bright yellow.

"Mrs. Robin has picked up a shell. She is carrying it into my hemlock hedge . . . and now she is back with a worm . . . a small, bright green one."

Tony turned to Mary Alice. "Wow, I'm glad to hear that. I was worried about the supply of baby-robin food in the Mayor's yard. Couldn't find one cabbage looper anywhere on Elm."

"Well, you're not a mother robin," Mary Alice said as she rose on her tiptoes and peered over Ginger's head.

"The new Cock Robin just came to the nest," the Mayor said. "He fed a baby!" A murmur went through the crowd.

The Deepening Disaster

"Long live the new Cock Robin!" Mayor Joe shouted. "He's got another worm—that looks like one from my lawn. Now Mrs. Robin is stepping down into the nest. She has spread feathers and wings and covered our babies.

"All's well in Saddleboro! The Cock Robin Day picnic has begun!"

Cheers went up, a drum rolled, a trumpet blasted off key, and above the din Tony heard the Mayor say something about this being the moment Saddleboro would take the lead in the national fight against pollution. But nobody was listening. The babies had hatched and that was all that mattered.

Tony said "See you" to Mary Alice, straddled his bike, pressed down on the pedals, and maneuvered across the Commons. He sped across Pine Street and down Crow Hill Road to the sewage-disposal plant, a huge, windowless square of cinder block and an acre of filters. Leaving his bike, he walked up the river until he was far above the plant, then took a water test. "Well, I'll be darned," he said aloud. The paper was deep green. He felt discouraged, then realized he knew something—that the mysterious chemical was not coming out of the disposal plant. He returned to his bike and went home.

Tony found his mother singing in the kitchen as she packed their tote-in–tote-out bag.

She told him that Mrs. Korkner was going to go to the picnic with them. Tony's eyes widened in surprise, for Mrs. Korkner, an elderly widow, had campaigned against the Mayor when he proposed a sewage-disposal plant. She had also campaigned against the school annex and other town improvements that raised her taxes. She called them threats to the elderly who lived on small pensions like hers. Tony's father had agreed with her except for one point. Hers was not a small pension. She had stock in the Missatonic Mill.

"Mrs. Korkner really loved Cock Robin," Tony's mother said. "She wants to go to his picnic, so I asked her to join us."

The back door opened and Tony's father came in, grumbling about having an emergency plumbing job on Cock Robin Day.

"We all set?" he asked as he went to the closet for his boccie ball.

Tony walked as far as the front gate with his parents and Mrs. Korkner, told them he had a job to do before the picnic, and dashed across the road, over the stone fence, and into the meadow. He found his well-worn trail to the marsh, wound through the cattails, and took a test in the open water. Once again the card turned bright green. Whatever the chemical was, it was all over Saddleboro.

Tony walked thoughtfully through the new woods the Mayor's Administration had added to the park and arrived at the picnic just as the Mayor was dipping a champagne glass into the Missatonic River. Holding it high, Mayor Joe carried it to the speaker's platform and opened the festivities by announcing that soon the citizens of Saddleboro would not only swim and fish in the beautiful Missatonic again, but drink from it.

Mayor Joe then said the Governor had called him and promised that for every dollar Saddleboro raised for a detergent filter on the disposal plant, the state would match it with two. Mrs. Korkner shouted that she would rather use soap. Mary Alice and her friend Ginger seconded this, and the kids shouted, "Soap, soap." Tony barely heard them, he was so angry. He wanted to shout, "You're all wrong!" but the words did not come out. Disillusioned by the Mayor, disgusted by his own stage fright, he dug a hole in the ground with his heel and resolved once and for all that he *would* find who killed Cock Robin. He had been asked to do so, and he would, whether the Mayor liked it or not.

The protest died down. The Mayor made a few heartfelt remarks about the beauty of the baby robins, and left the podium. Lunch boxes were opened and the picnic began. The band played "America," and Mrs. Korkner buttonholed Mayor Joe as he came smiling by. She asked if the filter would raise her taxes. He said something vague and strode toward the baseball field. Tony glanced at the bees and then at the thunderhead that was now moving close to the sun. The mill foreman, Wally Piekartz, threw an armload of baseball bats on the field and Mayor Joe turned back just before he stepped on a bee-filled anthill. Tony said, "Darn, he should have gotten stung, then he'd look at the problems in Saddleboro." But nobody was listening.

"Look at those bees!" Wally exclaimed. "And the ants!" He rubbed his head. "Darned if I don't have them all over my place, too." Tony made a mental note of this rather than pulling out his notebook. He was embarrassed to write in front of people for fear they would think him odd. He stepped off the diamond as Mary Alice came wandering through the crowd and joined him. She, too, saw the bees, giggled, and nudged Tony.

"Who's going to play baseball in a bee field?"

Tony squinted at the sky.

"No one," he said as a cloud engulfed the sun. "We've been saved by a shadow."

By the time Wally and his son had brought the mitts and balls to the diamond the bees were gone. The cloud cover was just enough to put the light threshold so low that the bees could not see well enough to hunt. They vanished, leaving the field to the ants and the players.

Tony played shortstop in a long, noisy game that the other team won. When it was over the band struck up a polka and Tony sat down to watch the ants being hammered into their dwellings by dancing feet.

Around ten P.M. Tony and his parents packed up their trash and went home. At the back door his father opened the garbage can and dumped the tote bag.

"Makes me feel good," he said. "Never could stand that park after a picnic. Maybe we've learned something." As they went inside, the thunder rumbled and the rain began to fall. Tony took out his notebook, made a note about the ants in Wally Piekartz' yard, and jotted down the time of the storm.

"Perfect timing," said Mr. Isidoro and closed the kitchen door.

As Tony lay in bed he pondered events and felt more kindly toward the Mayor. Two baby robins sat under their mother in his funny hat across the street. Duckweed grew once more in the Missatonic River and everyone at the picnic had toted out their trash. Saddleboro might, after all, be leading the nation in the fight against pollution. He was smiling as he dropped off to sleep.

In the morning Tony got the paper before his father, opened it, and read the headline: A SPOTLESS PARK AT MIDNIGHT. IT CAN BE DONE. Under David Lowenthal's byline was the story of his midnight walk through the park with a flashlight. "The sewageless river purled in the darkness," he wrote. "The trees rustled. Not even a pop-top could be found. Bravo Saddleboro." Tony felt good about David Lowenthal, too.

Since Mayor Joe did not broadcast until ten o'clock on Sunday, Tony turned the radio on low at nine forty-five and tried to phone Rob. He did not answer at either the lab or his room. Knowing how precise scientists were and how careful they must be about their findings, he tried to be patient and settled down to his homework.

Who Really Killed Cock Robin?

The phone rang. It was the Mayor. He wanted to know if there were any natural causes for the death of baby robins. Tony suggested crows, bluejays, snakes, and raccoons, then asked him to hang on while he checked his brother's notes. A few minutes later he told the Mayor that out of two broods of 5 eggs that robins generally have, about 3.6 survive. The Mayor thanked him and hung up before Tony could ask him why he wanted the information. He suspected, however, that one of Cock Robin's babies was in danger, went to his room, and turned his binoculars on Mrs. Robin. He could see nothing to alarm him, for she was sitting on the nest. At ten o'clock he turned on the kitchen radio.

"Citizens of Saddleboro," the Mayor began. "We've proven that people can gather, have fun, and clean up. Town Park is immaculate. Thank you." His voice was not as jubilant as usual and Tony soon learned why. "It's with sadness I announce the death of one of the baby robins. It died during the night. Mrs. Robin carried it out at five-thirty when I was watering my lawn and dropped it near the marsh." He cleared his throat and went on to say that he had done some research and found that mortality is naturally high in young birds. He then repeated what Tony had told him.

"But we have three eggs," he said. "Do not be discouraged. Cock Robin will yet beat the average and four beautiful offspring will fly in the bright air of Saddleboro."

The Deepening Disaster

Mayor Joe did not link the death of the baby robin to detergents.

Tony turned off the radio, went down to the garage for his bike, and rode out the highway past the farms and fields. About two miles from home he parked by the iron bridge that crossed the Missatonic and walked down to the water. He dipped the chlorinated hydrocarbon card. It turned a black green—a violent reaction. He was elated. Somewhere nearby the mysterious chemical was seeping into the river.

Glancing around, he looked for a possible source—a mill, a barn, a human dwelling. There was none that he could see, only trees and rolling hills. He got back on his bike, snooped down a dirt road, but found nothing and pedaled swiftly back to Saddleboro.

At home he took out Izzy's maps and put them on the floor. Discarding the wind map, he studied the one labeled "human habitations."

"Ah-ha!" he exclaimed. The town dump lay behind a ridge not far from the bridge. This seemed a real possibility for contamination until he noticed that the dump was not on the watershed of the Missatonic. The land drained to the north, not into the river. He flipped through Izzy's file on the dump, found it no help, turned to the one on the park. If he could not find out where the mysterious chemical was coming from, he might at least turn up a clue that would explain why there were so many ants in the field. He went through the lists of catbirds, song sparrows, and cardinals that had nested there, found nothing pertinent, gave up, and went downstairs for a piece of pie. As he spooned ice cream on it he thought about the park. All the bushes where the birds had nested had been cleaned out by the kids for the picnic. If there were no birds to eat ants, the ants would multiply. He was about to check and see if these birds ate ants when a song on the radio was interrupted for a special announcement. Mary Alice came on the air.

"Hi," she said. "I am at the Mayor's house with a new organization called Friends of Cock Robin. We have a name for his baby. Ginger Pierce wants to call him Robbie after his father, but seven of us want to call him Saddle. After all, he *is* Saddleboro's Clean Environment bird."

Tony sat down. By naming the baby robin, he too became a personality, and that was bad. If he did not live, Mayor Joe would probably invent another killer and confuse everything more, and Tony was beginning to believe that Saddle might not survive. If something was the matter with three eggs and one nestling, then something was probably wrong with Saddle. Mary Alice, with her usual poise, described the baby—his tufts of down, his funny, featherless wings that looked like penguin paddles, and his knobby bald head. She urged all the children to tell their parents not to use detergents. "Thousands of birds died in Florida this spring because of pollution," she said. "We mustn't let that happen here."

The Mayor said "Good living" and tried to sign off, but Mary Alice got in the last word. "Saddle is so good that everyone should clean up and try to help him. He doesn't even cry. He just opens his little red mouth when he's hungry."

With that Tony rushed downstairs to the phone and tried to reach Rob again. He still did not answer, so Tony dialed the Mayor.

"Sir," he said, "I think something's wrong with Saddle!"

"What do you mean?" he shouted.

"I've been listening to Mary Alice. Saddle's one day old and hasn't made a peep. He should be giving the food call, a loud, noisy squawk."

"Wait a minute—I'll ask Ellen if she's heard it." Tony could hear him calling to his wife. There was a long pause and the Mayor was back on the phone to say she hadn't heard him cry at all. "What does that mean?"

"I'm not sure. But it isn't normal. Nestlings scream when their parents come to feed them."

The Mayor groaned.

"Tony, Saddle just can't die. What'll we do?"

Tony had no answer.

"Also," Mayor Joe said in a discouraged voice, "I didn't tell the girls this, but I haven't seen Mrs. Robin for hours."

"I'll call you back," Tony said, hung up, and went to Izzy's room. He looked through his files for the formula he used for feeding baby birds, couldn't find it, and asked his mother if she remembered it. She did indeed, having mixed it for a nestling Izzy brought home only a year ago.

The phone rang. Tony hoped it was Rob, but it was Mayor Joe again.

"Tony, do robins ever get new mothers? I mean, *two* foster parents?"

"Yes."

"Thank heavens. I'll just wait and watch for a new mother. I think Mrs. Robin is dead. I haven't seen her since breakfast."

"Oh, gee! I'll check and call you back." Tony hung up, dashed out the front door, leaped over his hedge, and then the stone fence at the edge of the meadow. Beginning at the top of the hill, he walked down to the edge of the marsh and then back, spacing his return about three feet away. In this manner he slowly covered every inch of ground as he searched for Mrs. Robin. After an hour he came to one of the springs that fed the marsh. He was ready to give up when he saw a feather twisting in the breeze about six feet out in a patch of watercress. Wading to it, he picked up the tan breast feathers of a female robin, as well as several flight and tail feathers. Tony looked at the sky and waited for the culprit to appear, for he recognized the work of the marsh hawk. When after fifteen minutes neither the male nor the female flew over, he worried. This was the hour of the day they hunted.

Taking off at full speed, he crossed the road and

darted into the woods where the hawks had nested ever since he could remember.

They were not at their nest, and it did not look used. Sticks hung loosely from the edges and there were no white marks from young birds that indicate their presence. He went on through the woods, checking every large nest he saw, for occasionally marsh hawks move. When he did not find them he wondered if they had been eating sick birds like Mrs. Robin, had accumulated poisons, and died. Chlorinated hydrocarbons like DDT and metals eaten by one animal are passed on to the next in the food chain until eventually the predators such as hawks, owls, and eagles get lethal doses and die. And without the predators to control the birds that control the insects, trouble is upon the land.

About three o'clock Tony rapped on the Mayor's back door.

"Bad news, eh?" Mayor Joe said as Tony showed him the feathers.

"It's Mrs. R., all right," he said. "I found these feathers within her territory. No other female would trespass on her land. Males teach their mates the boundaries of their property and they stay within them."

"Who killed her?"

"The marsh hawk, I think. Feathers were pulled out and scattered around. A cat or fox doesn't pluck; they kill and carry."

"Shoot him! Shoot him!" the Mayor shouted.

"No!" Tony said. "Besides, he may already be dead.

I can't find him. Furthermore, something was the matter with Mrs. Robin. I found her feathers out in the watercress. No robin normally goes into an environment like that. Watercress is for herons and wading birds. You may say she was carried there by the hawk, but she wasn't. She was killed where I found the feathers. I could see the impact points where the hawk's wings struck the cress."

The Mayor sat down on the steps, put his head in his hands, and told Tony that the male had not been feeding Saddle. "He's just singing from the hickory and spruce tree. Singing, singing."

"He's trying to attract another female and if Saddle doesn't give the food call, it's very likely he'll die. The sound is important. The parents must hear this cry. It makes them feed the young. Has he cried yet?"

"No. And the other eggs haven't hatched."

"They won't at this late date. Something's wrong. Can I take them to the lab at the college for analysis? I have a friend there who's a histochemist. If he can find out what chemicals are in the eggs—he says Cock Robin probably died of chemical poisoning—then we can find the source, catch the offender, and stop more deaths."

This time the Mayor did not say no. Instead he opened the door and led Tony through the house to the front porch where the nest sat neatly in the crown of his Stetson. "Take them," the Mayor said, "but don't hurt Saddle."

As Tony picked up the three eggs, the Mayor rubbed his cheek and sighed.

"Tony, will Saddle die tonight without a mother?"

"He hasn't got much chance if he's not fed and brooded." The little bird felt the disturbance at the nest, lifted his wobbly head, and opened his beak.

"He's got to live," the Mayor said sadly. "I like him."

"He's got a chance if we hand-raise him, but it takes devotion and time."

"Can you do it?"

"Not if I'm going to find out who killed Cock Robin . . . and I am."

"Who could?"

"Mary Alice."

"But she has to go to school."

"You could write her a note. Ask the nuns if she could keep Saddle in the teachers' room and be excused every twenty minutes to feed him. I've got a food formula for young birds."

The Mayor suggested they wait a few hours to see if a foster mother arrived, but Tony shook his head. "There're not enough robins in Saddleboro to take the chance." He picked up the tiny bird and brooded it in his hands. The Mayor rushed to his phone and called Mary Alice.

She arrived within the minute, her hair flying as her flashing feet tapped the sidewalk. When she had caught her breath, Tony explained to her what she must do.

They crossed the street, found Mrs. Isidoro in the garden, and Tony asked if she would mix some of her formula for a baby robin. When eggs, raw meat, and cereal were wetted down with yeast and water, Tony jiggled his hand above Saddle's head. The tiny bird opened his mouth, Tony dropped a morsel in it, and Saddle swallowed.

"He'll eat for us. That's good," Tony said. "Some little birds won't. They have to be force-fed and that's hard on them. They usually die."

He then told Mary Alice to keep Saddle warm at night with a light bulb and feed him about every twenty minutes by day. Mrs. Isidoro lined a shoe box with face tissues and Mary Alice went out the door gingerly carrying her precious charge.

As soon as she departed Tony wrapped the robin eggs in paper napkins, put them in his knapsack, and biked to the college. Rob was not in the lab, so he left the eggs and a note.

> Rob: Mrs. R. is dead. These eggs, as you can plainly see, haven't hatched. Saddle is not acting normal. The marsh hawk is gone. There aren't many birds in the Saddleboro Marsh. We're in trouble.
>
> Tony

Before he went to bed that night he carefully copied a chart. It was the day-by-day development of song-bird nestlings from the hour they hatch until they fly on the ninth or tenth day. He took it from the volume by the scientist Margaret Morse Nice, entitled *Studies in the Life History of the Song Sparrow.* Izzy had checked the chart with the nestlings in the Isidoro apple tree last spring and found it exactly pertained to robins.

Before school the next morning he took the copy to Mary Alice and told her to compare Saddle's behavior and development with the list. Any deviation, he emphasized, would indicate trouble.

"Is this Dr. Isidoro's Baby Manual?" she asked.

"Mrs. Nice's," he answered.

The next day Tony walked to school by way of Mary Alice's house and checked on Saddle. He was surprised to find him alive. Even the healthiest baby birds were difficult to raise, and Saddle was not the most perfect specimen.

On the fifth day Saddle was not only alive, but preening his feathers—exactly on schedule. He still did not call for food and Tony wondered if he had a voice at all. Without one, he would not live long in the wilds, for robins depend on their voices to locate friends, establish land borders, and warn of enemies.

On the seventh day, he was pleased to see that Saddle was still on schedule. He could get off his heels, stand on his toes, and stretch his wings. This was such good news that he decided to drop by the Mayor's office at lunchtime and tell him that perhaps Saddle would fly free in Saddleboro after all.

The Mayor was not in a pleasant mood, Tony learned

from his secretary as she handed him the *Capital News*. An editorial circled in red pencil said the Governor was considering a Jim Rockwell to fill the vacancy in the state senate and that Joe Dambrowski of Saddleboro had lost a great deal of prestige when Cock Robin died. Letters were pouring in to the Governor joking facetiously about the "poor bird" who had been killed by detergents in a town where the administrator was a conservationist.

The Mayor's door opened, he stormed out of his room, saw Tony, and stopped.

"What's the phone number of that friend of yours, the histochemist at the college? I need an informed scientist." He paused. "Frank Lamberty just called and said I killed Cock Robin with weed killers. I've never used them. He's just retaliating for having to buy that truck to dump his dyes. His kid and those Friends of Cock Robin are accusing me; and I need scientific facts to stop them."

Tony read off Rob's telephone number as the Mayor dialed. He got no answer, and fuming told Tony he had better get back to school.

Tony went out the door and slid down the banister to the first floor. He crossed the street, walked into the parochial school, and made his way through kids returning from lunch to the teachers' room. Mary Alice was holding food above Saddle's head.

"Tony!" she said. "Look! Saddle's hopping. He's right on schedule." She put him on the table and chirped to him. He hopped over magazines and books, jumped to her fingers, and perched on her wrist. Then he fluttered to her shoulder, pecked a wisp of her hair, and begged for food. While she fed him Mrs. Isidoro's formula, Tony suggested that she not accuse anyone of the death of Cock Robin until the report came in from the lab. "It could be your father," he said.

"How could it be?" she asked, her brows puckering. "Daddy may have killed fish in the river, but not Cock Robin. I told you he hasn't dumped dyes since way back in March."

She sat down and stared at Tony with a hurt expression on her face.

"Why did you say that? Gee, Tony, I thought we were friends." He did not answer. She dropped her head and rubbed her hands pensively on her knees, then Saddle pecked her ear and she laughed. Swinging around, she looked up at Tony again.

"You know, you're not the only detective," she said tartly. "The Friends of Cock Robin have been doing some snooping, too. We have found people burning trash, DDT in six garages, and all kinds of fungicides in the Mayor's tool shed. He calls them Nature's Powders."

"Fungicides?" Tony said curiously.

"Yes. It's written on the bags, FUNGICIDE—FOR GREENER LAWNS."

"I don't know what's in them. Do you?"

"No, but I'm sure they aren't good. Anyway, my

father did *not* kill Cock Robin, and you are despicable to even think so. Get lost, Tony Isidoro!"

Tony walked out the door and back to school. He considered going to the lab to talk to Rob, but remembered that tests took time and that Rob had promised to call as soon as he knew anything.

4. Clues

Tony was awakened by silence early the next morning. The new Cock Robin was not singing and the quiet broke into his sleep. He stepped to his window and saw the male on the Mayor's freshly watered green lawn. Beside him hopped a female. He sighed. At least *that* problem was solved. The silence was not the death of another robin but the new male's preoccupation with a dusty tan female who must have come north on the last wave of the migration. He wondered why she was so late. Had something held her up to the south? It seemed that one solution only led to more mysteries.

Tony leaned on the windowsill watching the robins when he saw a bush tremble and Rob came around the Mayor's tool shed carrying sections of piping, a saw, and an auger used to take soil samples. Tony dressed in less than a minute and met him near the stone fence.

"Tone!" Rob said. "I was coming to get you." He slapped him on the back, looked down Elm, remarked that it was good to be back on his old stomping ground, and told Tony to sit down.

Rob settled himself beside him on the grass, took the knapsack off his back, and got out his notebook.

"Let me fill you in on the report. Cock Robin did have DDT in his tissues—but not enough to kill him. Still, it's an important factor, and since we haven't been using it in Saddleboro I asked Craig to find out where it came from. He began with his air snooper and the last date you heard frogs. He discovered talcum, like ladies' talcum powder, in his mid-April samples. The talcum was full of DDT. He called a manufacturer and found they use talc to make the DDT heavy and bring it to earth. More tests showed heavy doses fell on Saddleboro County the week Cock Robin arrived. Now Craig's calling all the manufacturers to find out who bought large quantities of DDT around here at that time. It didn't kill Cock Robin, but it may have killed something in the food chain.

"Meanwhile you and I have to find the source of that green chemical on your test card. Cock Robin had a dose of it—turned my test card green. But I don't know what it is. Neither does the Fish and Wildlife Service Research Station in Maryland. They've found it in fish and birds. So have the scientists at the Scripps Institution in California. It acts very much like DDT, attacks the fat around nerve tissues, and makes eggshells so thin they break. But no one knows what it is. If we can track it down we can name it. It's certainly as deadly to wildlife as DDT, and *is* another chlorinated hydrocarbon.

"There was also some mercury in old C.R. I don't know where that's coming from either. In addition, he had the usual dose of lead from gasoline that washes into the ground, is absorbed by the plants, gets into fruits and berries, and hence to Cock Robin."

Tony shook his head. "Wow! Poor bird." Rob nodded.

"Any clues about the source of the mystery chemical?" he asked.

Tony reported that it was in the marsh and the river above the sewage plant and heavy in the Missatonic below the iron bridge. Rob scratched his head. "Sounds as if it's airborne." He stroked his beard. "Can't be. Craig didn't pick it up in the snooper. Neither have the Scripps people found it in the air."

"Well, then how did it get to the marsh?" Tony asked. "The river doesn't flow through it."

"That's true."

"What's between Saddleboro and the bridge?"

"The dump."

"That means the air again. The dump doesn't drain

into the river. But it just can't be." Tony did not know what to say. The investigation seemed at an end before it began.

"Let's check out the marsh," Rob said. "We've got something to go on there. The fish died for some reason and the note you left me said there're not many frogs and that the hawks are missing. Also, the marsh is close to the spot where Cock Robin died."

Rob got up and Tony followed him over the stone fence into the meadow. Neither talked, both pondered. When they came to the aspens and willows at the edge of the Saddleboro Marsh, Tony led Rob down his trail through the cattails to the waving acres of marsh grasses. Beyond the grass were plants that like their feet in the water. Rob pulled up a bullrush, took out his hand lens, and examined the algae that grew on it.

"Just as I thought: a green algae." Tony wanted to know what that meant and Rob explained that the water was too rich. Nitrogen from some source has killed the normal blue-green algae community, a sort of town of one-celled plants and microscopic animals that must have pure water. If not, they die. "When they die this 'sewer weed' that thrives on nitrogen comes in." Tony reminded him that there were no sewer openings near the marsh and Rob explained that fertilizers could do the same thing. They contain nitrogen. The Everglades National Park, he went on, was a prime example of farm fertilizers one hundred miles north killing the blue-green algae in the park. This lowly community is vital to the glades. It precipitates the calcium out of the water, the calcium forms a mud-like marl essential to the growth of the sawgrass that fills the glades. The sawgrass dies and makes peat. In the peat grow cypresses, willows, mahoganies, and other beautiful trees that house bird, beast, and bug. Without the blue-green algae, the cycle is doomed. Saddleboro Marsh, Rob explained, was almost as delicate. Without its blue-green algae community, there would be no black bog soil in which the reeds, rushes, and cattails grew. "Weeds would spring up everywhere in and out of the water, change the soil, the soil would change the plants, and the creatures of the wetlands would vanish."

"Too much nitrogen, huh?" Tony said. "So the farmer is killing the marsh by fertilizing the meadow above it?"

"Perhaps. Does he fertilize it?"

"I've never seen him. But I'll ask."

Tony noticed a brownish-yellow scum on the surface beyond the water lilies. He pointed it out to Rob, who snapped his fingers.

"Dead plants. The marsh *is* dying from too much fertilizer. That's it, Tone! The blue-green algae is gone. The green algae has grown, used up the oxygen, and killed the floating water plants. They decomposed, or oxidized, as we call it, a process like that of a fire that burns oxygen and releases carbon dioxide. They took more oxygen from the water. So it's a lack of oxygen that killed the fish that attracted the gulls. If we can find out where that fertilizer is coming from, we'll know who's killing the marsh—and possibly Cock Robin. Although the damage is in the marsh, it *might* have affected him indirectly through the food chain."

Tony offered to show Rob where most of the fish had died, hoping they might find fertilizer there. They walked through the clattering rushes until they came to a weatherbeaten dock.

"Hey," Rob said. "Izzy and I built this years ago. Used to fish off it. Caught huge bass." He tested the structure with his foot; it teetered so much he crawled out on all fours, then stretched out on his stomach and reached down into the water. Scooping up a handful of mud, he slopped it on the dock and looked through it.

"The marsh *is* dying," he said. "There are very few insect larvae, and the little lobster-like copepods are nil."

"My big fish is gone!" Tony called as he curled his shoulders and head under the dock. "There was a four-teen-inch large-mouth bass here in April. I don't see him."

Rob leaned back on the wharf and looked across the water.

"Okay. We know why the fish died," he said, "but I can't understand the missing frogs. They don't need oxygen in the water. They're air breathers. You say the Mayor uses a fungicide?"

"I said Mary Alice said that the Mayor had fungicide in his shed."

"How about weed killers?"

"I don't know. Why?"

Rob said that the weed killer 2,4,5–T created birth deformities in young mammals and even human babies. He explained that although it had been banned on agricultural land by the U.S. government, it could still be used on range, forest, and pasture.

Tony sat up.

"Gee, Saddle doesn't cry. Do you think that's the reason why?"

"Could be."

"Maybe he *does* use weed killers," Tony said.

Rob scanned the wharf pilings for water snails, then asked Tony if he had made a count of the marsh birds recently and compared it with Izzy's notes. Tony shook his head, cupped his hand behind his ears, and listened. The water lapped and the gnats hummed around his head. A mallard called from somewhere in the cove. Presently he heard one black duck, a few red-winged blackbirds, and a marsh wren.

"That's a poor showing," said Rob. "This place used to sound like a full orchestra in May—grebes called, herons squawked, blackbirds rasped, and the frogs and toads trilled and piped."

Tony recalled that he had seen a great blue heron a few days ago, but had thought it a migrant because it departed with beeline determination. "You know how they head north and fly hard."

"The marsh will soon be a grave," Rob said. "Look

at these weed trees." He pointed to junipers and gray birch that were replacing the cattails and reeds.

They got up to leave. At the end of the wharf Rob sawed down a juniper and counted the rings.

"Four years old," he said. "Four years ago nitrogen began creeping into this marsh, making way for the weeds.

"Where *is* it coming from?" He scanned the Mayor's property, Tony's, the town itself. "I'd say Mayor Joe's, except the rain that carries the fertilizer off his lawn runs downhill to the river, not the marsh."

Tony remembered Izzy's map of the soils and rocks of Saddleboro, and suggested Rob look at it.

"The rocks are strange," he said. "Limestone, I think."

"Limestone? Oh-ho! Limestone doesn't always move water the way you'd expect. I think we'd better put a little marker on the Mayor's lawn—a yellow dye the Navy developed to mark the sea."

Tony got the idea. The Mayor's watering would wash the dye down the drainage route and tell them where his fertilizers finally came to rest.

Tony didn't think tracing a fertilizer was helping him with his job of finding out who killed Cock Robin and said as much to Rob.

"It's just as much a crime to kill this marsh as a robin. Maybe more so, when you consider how many wild plants and animals live here that keep Saddleboro clean."

They went home via the hawk woods. The nest was

still empty. As they walked back through the field, Tony noticed another outbreak of ants. He pointed them out to Rob and asked if he thought they had multiplied because there were so few birds. Rob thought not.

"I'll take a soil sample," he said, pushing his auger into the ground near an anthill. "Maybe an analysis of the earth will tell us something. Could be too acid, not enough lime, could be lack of nitrogen—there are some natural causes for outbreaks of insects."

Tony collected a pair of ground spiders to add to his terrarium while Rob twisted the auger into the ground.

At Tony's gate he asked when the Mayor watered his lawn and Tony recalled that he was usually sprinkling around six in the evening and again before sunup. Rob thought they had better put the dye on his lawn after dark so the morning sprinkling would carry it away. He then suggested they check the town dump Saturday morning. "Just in case the mysterious chemical is somehow coming from there. It's the only man-made thing anywhere near the bridge." He shook his head. "But how does it get to the water?"

Tony heard the school bell ring, dashed into his house for his books, and out the back door.

At nine P.M. he heard Rob whistle, opened his window, and climbed down the rainspout. They met by the Mayor's hemlock hedge, stole silently into his yard, and spread the sea marker. The Mayor and Mrs. Dambrowski were entertaining guests and their laughter easily drowned out the noise of the sticks Tony snapped as he followed Rob through the garden to the stone fence and the street. He did not worry about their being heard. At his gate he told Rob he would see him at dawn and crawled back up the rainspout. He had just finished his homework and watered his terrarium when the phone rang and he went downstairs to answer it.

"Tone, this is Rob. I'm at the lab. Craig just came in to say that they picked up that mysterious chemical on the air snooper the night of Cock Robin Day. Remember it rained? Well, it came down in the rain! Apparently it doesn't show in the air, but it's there. He turned on the sprinklers today and found it again. So the dump's a good hunch. If it's in the air and combines with water, the river would get the dose during this dry spring; so would the marsh. Bring that soil map of Izzy's tomorrow. Dr. Melvin says your end of town has underground rivers."

Before dinner on Thursday Tony was watching the pair of spiders he brought back from the ant outbreak near the hawk woods when he heard voices across the street and hurried to the window. Mayor Joe, Mary Alice, Saddle, and a photographer were on the porch. Mary Alice seemed upset but the photographer looked elated as he snapped pictures of the hat and empty nest. Tony, curious about Saddle, whom he had not seen since the day before yesterday, ran down his back steps and out the kitchen door. He crossed to the meadow and slipped into the Mayor's hemlock hedge. Picking his way through the twisted trunks, he settled himself on the ground, where he could peer through the hedge at the porch. Saddle was apparently a real showman. He was sitting on Mary Alice's head.

"A little more to the right," the photographer said. The Mayor stepped beside her. "Not you, sir. I'll get you later." The camera clicked, the Mayor paced the porch, Saddle fluttered from Mary Alice's head to the photographer's, lost his footing, and landed on the porch. As Mary Alice picked him up the man asked her who really killed Cock Robin.

"Several people," she snapped. "My friends and I have been doing some sleuthing. John Pierce, the hardware-store owner, has been spraying his garden with DDT at night. We found cans in his trash. And the Mayor . . ."

"Now, Mary Alice," interrupted Mayor Joe with forced laughter, "we'll soon have a reliable report from the State College." He turned to the photographer. "My Administration is investigating this scientifically," he said. "I realize the complexity of ecology, not conservation or pollution, but ecology, and I have turned the problem over to the scientists. The bird, the unhatched eggs, and the total ecosystem will be investigated. I'll make a statement when I have the facts."

"Is he ever going to fly in the clean Saddleboro air?" the photographer asked.

"Well, yes, as a matter of fact, he is. Next week

there'll be a Fly-Away ceremony on the Commons. I'm going to ask the Governor to come and I'll declare a holiday in Saddleboro. It will be a big day for the anti-pollution forces. TV will record the bird's flight and the whole nation will see what we have done in our town."

The photographer turned to Mary Alice; she was obviously better copy, but she said no more, for just then Mrs. Dambrowski came to the door and invited everyone in to tea. The photographer took one picture of the Mayor when Saddle flew to his shoulder and stuck his beak in his ear.

"He's giving you the devil for killing his pa," the photographer said with a wink and stepped into the house.

Mary Alice excused herself to Mrs. Dambrowski and rushed down the steps. Saddle fluttered from her wrist to her shoulder and Tony could see how well he balanced himself with his wings. Counting on his fingers, Tony figured the bird was nine days old and doing fine—making short flights and balancing. He was maturing on schedule, except for his voice. The last time he had seen him he thought he would not be able to balance well enough to fly. Now, he thought, he might fly in the "clean air" of Saddleboro for at least a few days.

Winding back through the hedge he crawled out on the sidewalk and started across the street as Mary Alice came through the gate and saw him.

"I'm glad to see you," she said eagerly. "Something's wrong with Saddle. I think we should free him right away, like tomorrow, so . . ."

"So you won't be the killer of Cock Robin Junior?"

"So Saddleboro won't be," she said indignantly.

"What's the matter with him?"

"He sleeps with his mouth open, and there's nothing in Margaret Nice's book to explain it."

"Do you still keep him under a light bulb at night?"

"Of course."

"Well, don't. He's got all his feathers and it's too hot for him. He's panting. Birds just open their mouths when they pant." Mary Alice pushed back her bangs and smiled with relief as Saddle fluttered to the ground and ran into the hedge. Tony scrambled after him, Mary Alice followed.

"Oooo," she said, as she looked around. "It's divine in here. Spooky and beautiful." As Tony crept through the limbs, Saddle hopped, Tony reached, Saddle hopped, and so they went to the end of the hedge, where dense needles blocked the bird. Tony carefully picked him up, tucked him in his shirt, and was wiggling onto the side-walk when something caught his eye, a bit of yellow cloth like the piece the first Mrs. Robin had woven into her nest. He stuffed it in his pocket and returned Saddle to Mary Alice.

By now word of the photographer had gotten around town and several high school kids were coming down Elm Street. The balloon launchers of the funeral day gathered at the Mayor's gate. The tallest asked Mary Alice if he could hold Saddle. She refused.

"Come on," the boy insisted, "or I'll tell the reporter who did kill Cock Robin." He reached for the bird. Mary Alice pulled away.

"Your old man killed him!" the boy shouted and reached again.

Tony stepped between them. "I wouldn't accuse anyone yet," he said.

"The villain's John Pierce!" another boy yelled and pushed John Pierce, Jr. "Your old man burns his trash."

John Junior shoved him back. "Why don't you clean up your car? Every time your pa drives past our house we put on gas masks."

"Yeah? Well, wait until the Health Board gets you for busted sewer pipes. The whole neighborhood will get sick because of you!" John Junior shouldered him and the boy struck out, but the tall kid grabbed his fist before it contacted. He lost it and was pummeled in the stomach. When he slugged back with a blow to the chin, the other kids joined the fracas. Tony grabbed Saddle from Mary Alice's shoulder and pulled her across the street.

As he reached the gate Saddle peered up at him and tried to struggle free. Tony held him more firmly and as he did so Saddle gave forth a loud distress cry. He screamed again and again. Tony was so elated he did not hear the squad car until it stopped in front of the

Mayor's house. Sergeant Sears jumped out, elbowed his way into the middle of the fight, and picked up John Pierce, Jr., by the back of his collar and the seat of his pants. He set him down on the curb, spun around, and lifted the instigator off his feet. Helplessly flailing, the boy calmed down. The others moved back and the battle was over.

"This's awful!" Mary Alice cried. Tony was looking at Saddle.

"It's great. Saddle can yell. He may live after all."

Tony's mother, who had come to the door when the police car arrived, mumbled, "Boys, boys" and invited Mary Alice in for a cup of hot chocolate. Tony followed, wearing a grin so wide it lifted his ears. He put Saddle on the back of Mary Alice's chair and sat down to admire him. Once more the bird screamed. Tony moved away and Saddle calmed down, shook out his rumpled feathers, and fluttered his baby wings at Mary Alice.

"He's beautiful," Tony's mother said. "You've done a good job, Mary Alice. I've tried to raise baby birds my Izzy found. It's very difficult. Never did succeed."

"I really love him, Mrs. Isidoro," Mary Alice said. "I don't really ever want to let him go." Tears rose in her eyes. "The Mayor's going to set him free next week." She straightened her back and looked at the bubbles that floated on her chocolate.

"I think he just wants him out of his sight." Her

bottom lip trembled. "Because the whole thing's gotten out of hand—fights, accusations, police even." She pushed back her bangs and stirred her chocolate. Tony had never seen her so defenseless. He stirred his chocolate, too.

"There's a good side to it," Mrs. Isidoro said and sat down. "Everyone in Saddleboro knows more about pollution and robins than they ever did before. And we're still learning."

"We sure are!" Tony's father was standing in the doorway grinning.

"Wait until you hear about David Lowenthal," Mary Alice said. "The Friends of Cock Robin are going to tell what he's up to, and in his own paper—tomorrow." She explained that the club had done some "research," and decided to print their findings in the paper. "Mrs. Korkner said we better run it as an ad and gave us a check, but Mr. Lowenthal returned the check, saying he would run the ad as a letter-to-the-editor because he believes in publishing all sides of an issue."

"What's the big scoop?" Tony asked in surprise. "You really ought to wait for the college report."

"Not for this! Sis has given us a lot of news Mr. Lowenthal never printed, and we have found some of our own." She put her hand in back of Saddle's feet, he stepped on her finger, then she pushed back her chair and stood up.

"I guess it's time for me to go. I'm a detective, too, Tony Isidoro. Wait and see."

The next morning, Tony was awakened by the newspaper sliding across the porch. He ran outside in his pajamas and opened it. On the second page was a letter margined in black.

"Editor Lowenthal," it began, "The Friends of Cock Robin accuse *you* and the Mayor of his death."

"Wow!" Tony said aloud.

You did not report to your readers that Cock Robin was sick, although you and the Mayor knew it.

You did not report to your readers that sewage-disposal plants are not one hundred percent efficient, although you and the Mayor knew it.

You did not seek more reason than detergents for Cock Robin's death, although you use printer's ink, which is full of pollutants and the Mayor uses fungicides.

You have not been reporting people who are burning leaves.

You have not been reporting people who use DDT.

You have not named people who drop trash.

You have not cleaned up Saddleboro through good reporting.

Mary Alice Lamberty, President
Friends of Cock Robin

Tony heard his father coming down the steps.

"She's great," he called, and handed him the paper. "She ought to be Mayor."

Who Really Killed Cock Robin?

Mr. Isidoro read the letter, rubbed his moustache, and glanced across the page.

"Thought so," he said, and leaned back in his chair to read aloud Lowenthal's defense.

Dear Friends of Cock Robin:

I thank you for your letter. I plead guilty to all of your accusations, not, however, because I have withheld the news, but because I lacked knowledge in the field of ecology. What I did not know on May 18 is that a sick bird flips and jumps. Like Mayor Joe, I interpreted this as good spirits, although a young man named Tony Isidoro (credit where credit is due) warned us that the bird was ill. However, mayors and editors are not in the habit of quoting a twelve-year-old as a scientific source.

That was unfortunate.

As for the sewage-disposal plant, I *did* know it was not one hundred percent efficient, but that did not change my opinion. Eighty-percent effluence removal may not assure us of drinking water or the return of the trout, but it does assure swimming now and the return of the bass some day soon. As far as I'm concerned, the plant is a success!

Yes, Friends of Cock Robin, I did blame detergents because they are a pollutant. I realize now there are many more; lead, titanium, cadmium, printer's ink. We are all guilty.

86.

As for the burning of leaves and DDT—it looks as if I need more reporters. I will pay two cents a word for good news and feature stories, be you ten or sixty years old.

Since I am the editor, however, my judgment of newsworthiness is final.

And let me also say, the death of Cock Robin has proved to me how little I do know. Until we all understand man in relation to the food chain, and the balance of all plants and animals, we will continue to make mistakes. So I am enrolling in an ecology course at the State College. Would the Friends of Cock Robin like to join me? If you or anyone else in Saddleboro is interested, drop by my office and we'll make arrangements for a car pool.

The death of Cock Robin is more complex than we thought, and all the facts are not yet in.

Thank you, and say hello to Saddle for me.

David Lowenthal

Tony's father put down the paper and rocked back on his chair.

"I'm going to sign up for that course," he said. "That's where we've got to start—learning the laws of nature so we don't break them." He tossed his paper napkin toward the trash basket, it fell short and he jumped to his feet, picked it up, and put it in the container.

"Gets so a man can't even relax in his own home." He chuckled and stepped to the phone to call Lowenthal.

Tony picked up his books and walked out the back door, wishing that tomorrow's sun were rising and he had some facts.

5. The Dump

On Saturday Tony was waiting for Rob on the stone
fence that bordered the meadow. In the twilight before
dawn a soft mist crept up from the river and swirled
between the houses. As it enveloped Mrs. Korkner's
garden, an American toad trilled raucously and a male
robin sang from somewhere near the library. The
Mayor's robin answered him. Tony listened. No more
joined this first chorus of the birds and he was startled
to realize how few robins there were in Saddleboro. He
waited hopefully for the robin of the Town Park to
sing, but only the wind spoke from the river valley.

Tony glanced down Elm, did not see Rob, and went
to the hawk woods. He checked the nest, saw that it
was still empty, and returned through another field.
The thistles and yarrow that would blossom in summer

were barely above the ground, but the mustard plants were high and the clover dense. Tony wondered why this field was covered with green things and the next one was barren and riddled with ants. Then he heard Rob's bicycle clang against the stone fence, called "Hello" through the mist, and ran to meet him.

"Let's go!" Rob said. "It's the dump first."

Tony jumped over the wall and picked up his bike. As they pedaled west through the farm country, Rob steered his bike close to Tony's.

"Listen carefully," he said. "I've got a long story. Craig stopped by the lab last night to tell me that not long ago in Sweden Sören Jensen, a scientist, found a strange chemical in many fish and a dead eagle. It was so much like DDT that he called it an 'unknown but chlorine-containing compound.'

"A colleague of his, Gunnar Widmark, took a look at it, and together they identified it as PCB—polychlorinated biphenyl. No one knew much about it, but it worried the Swedes.

"The next year in America, Monte Kirven of the San Diego Natural History Museum found an unhatched egg in the nest of our next doomed species—the fabulous peregrine falcon—the bird of the kings. He took the egg to the lab of the Institute of Marine Resources in Berkeley for analysis. The tests showed that the egg contained five milligrams of DDE—the DDT compound that's the most abundant synthetic pollutant in the environment—and an abundance of another compound they couldn't identify.

"Next you brought us Cock Robin, then his eggs. After I looked at the embryo tissues I gave them to Craig because I was stumped by the mysterious chemical. He called a chemist friend at Berkeley who told us to test for polychlorinated biphenyls—PCBs. They were turning up in wildlife in Sweden, England, Scotland, the Netherlands, and that very day in the United States. I checked, because that's my field, and it *was* a PCB. Where do they come from? Almost everywhere. They're used as plasticizers, flame retardants, insulating fluids, in natural and synthetic rubber, electrical products, floor tiles, printer's ink, coatings for paper and fabric, varnishes, waxes, asphalt, and many adhesives and resins. The amounts being used are enormous."

Tony steered his bike closer.

"Manufacturers of PCBs," Rob went on, "know the stuff is dangerous. They protect their workers from it, but it has never occurred to them to ask whether PCB might be released into the environment and, if so, what it would do to birds, fish, and people.

"The Berkeley lab began looking for sources and located them in great quantities around industrial areas. No one is yet sure exactly where they're coming from, although they suspect the smokestacks of plants that manufacture PCB. Also industrial waste such as exhausts is another possible source because PCB, other synthetics, and oil are mixed together to make a fire-resistant hydraulic fluid. When this is used in industrial machines and engines, the PCBs escape into the air. Another source might be the weathering of PCB-containing products. This asphalt road, for instance, may contain PCB. If it does, every car that rolls over it erodes it and PCB enters the atmosphere."

Tony looked at the road with new eyes.

"Finally," Rob said, "many PCB products wind up in the city dumps, where they are burned and release highly toxic fumes.

"And now, here's what I'm leading up to. When we tested your green test card, it filtered out PCB. So it's all over Saddleboro, primarily in the river and marsh, but since that storm, it's now on the flowers and trees.

"I think we'll find the source in the dump. Perhaps some product that contains it is burning and putting it into the air."

"But no one burns at the dump any more. There's a town ordinance."

"That's why we're going there. I think someone is or has been burning a PCB product despite the fact there's a no-burn ordinance."

They wheeled silently for a mile as they climbed out of the Missatonic Valley into the foothills. The sun rose over the mountains and lit the fragile new leaves of the trees. Tony could hardly believe that unseen poisons floated over the golden hills. They seemed so perfect.

The Dump

As they passed a dairy farm, a flock of mallard ducks dropped over the trees. Their wings flashing, they alighted on a pond, paddled a moment, and took off. A few red-winged blackbirds called rusty territorial songs from the willows by the pond. Then the wood thrush trilled, and Tony decided the Earth was all right, until he remembered this was the first wood thrush he had heard this spring. Wood thrushes usually began singing every year on May 12, according to Izzy's notebook. Where were they?

At the dirt road that led into the Saddleboro dump, Tony slid off his bike seat and put his feet on the ground. The refuse was not visible, for it lay in a valley behind a ridge, but he knew it was there. He could smell it. The prevailing winds were drifting eastward toward him and Saddleboro. Rob leaned on his bike handles and studied the drift, then walked his bicycle to the top of the hill and rolled down.

"Let's go look," he said.

Tony followed him downhill, then up to the top of the ridge where he stopped and looked down on a midden of twentieth-century man. Engines and wheels, boxes and cartons, springs and mattresses, garbage and glass, plastics and synthetics, cans, tires, bottles, boilers, refrigerators, and newspapers were piled twenty feet high and acres wide.

"Beautiful," he said sarcastically.

"Strangely birdless," Rob answered. "Used to be

crows, blackbirds, and gulls here by the thousands."

They leaned their bikes against a dead oak and Rob walked around the tree, looking at the ground.

"Eight years ago," he said, "this dump was a half-acre hole surrounded by a woods." He took his knapsack off his back, opened his saddlebags, and pulled out a package. "An orchid called a pitcher plant once grew under this tree. Izzy and I collected them for a botanist at the college. The orchids are gone, the tree is dead, and the dump covers over ten acres. We are a very intelligent beast."

They crossed the packed area where the sanitation trucks backed up to dump, and paused on the edge of the mountain of waste. Pale fumes were rising from bound cartons and paper drums.

"Something *is* burning," Tony said as a rat came toward him. He kicked it, it rose to its hind feet, then calmly slinked between a boiler and a mat of greasy rags.

"He's sick," Tony said, as he moved away. "He's so bold."

Rob took a roll of wet gauze out of a vial and handed one end to Tony. "Go down the pile on that side of the fire. I'll go down here. We'll hold the tape over the fumes and pick up some of the particles. I'm hoping the wetness will precipitate out the PCB, if this is where it's coming from."

Tony eased himself from a crate to a tire, leaped over a bag of garbage, and balanced on the top of a kitchen range. Rob signaled him not to go any farther.

"This stuff is burned out underneath!" he called.

As Rob rolled in the tape, Tony saw him grab a tire and hang on. Then the entire side of the pile buckled and slid like a river of lava. Rob disappeared from view and the range began to sink under Tony. He jumped to a cardboard drum, his foot went through, and, as he pulled it out, a cloud of foul-smelling gas erupted and enveloped him. His eyes smarted. He leaped, lost his balance, gained it, and scrambled to the top of the dump on all fours. A half-burned piece of yellow cloth lay near his hand. He stuffed it in his pocket and ran across the packed area to look for Rob. When he saw him running safely around the bottom of the dump he closed his eyes. They were smarting so badly he could hardly see.

After a few minutes he felt better, opened his eyes, and saw Rob staggering toward him.

"Phew!" Rob said, "that was close. It was hot as Hades under there. But I think we've got what we came for." He held up the tape. "Let's go."

By the time they reached the highway, the morning traffic was moving and the mist had vanished with the sun. At the edge of the Lindquist farm, Rob rubbed his eyes.

"Tony! How do you feel?"

"I sting!"

"So do I. The river's close to the road here. Let's wash this stuff off." Suddenly Tony felt prickly all over. He dropped his bike, jumped the fence, and ran.

Rob, close on his heels, ripped off his knapsack and shirt, passed Tony, and leaped into the water in pants and shoes. Tony plunged in after him with all his clothes on. Sinking to the bottom, he undressed, scrubbed his face, his chest and legs, then surfaced with a roar. He saw Rob treading water, head under as he washed his hair, his ears, and back. Finally Rob blew like a seal and looked up.

"Whatever it is, it's terrible." He washed his face again, swam to the shallows, and sat on the muddy bottom.

"Now what do we do?" Tony said. "We can't go back naked, and we can't put on our clothes."

"I've got a change in my saddlebags. You can wear the shirt. I'll wear the pants." Tony shivered, walked to the shore, dashed to the fence, reached over it, and got Rob's saddlebags. He came back to the river bank and they half-dressed. Rob commented that if Tony rode on his shoulders, between the two of them they'd be one well-dressed man.

Tony was eager to see if the marker on the Mayor's lawn had reached the marsh, but Rob told him to change his clothes, for there was no hurry. It could take several days.

Mrs. Isidoro was up when Tony went to his room to change his clothes, and he called to her that he and Rob would be back for breakfast in about an hour.

"I'll have muffins and sausage and Rob's favorite omelet," she answered cheerfully. Tony took the yellow fabric out of his wet clothes, wrapped them in a newspaper, and stuffed them under his work table. He joined Rob, who was ambling toward the meadow, and gave him back his shirt. Rob put it on as they hurried toward the wharf.

The water around it showed no sign of yellow marker.

Rob was just about to go back to the lab, but Tony suggested they first go to the cove where he had seen the herring gulls eating the dead fish. He led the way, jumping from one grass hummock to the next until he came to a dense stand of cranberries. The line of least resistance was through the water, and Tony splashed in without hesitating. The green algae thickened and Rob commented that they were approaching some kind of pollution. The peat on the bottom began to shake and sink; they clambered ashore, tramped through cattails, steeplebush, and bullrush, and burst out upon a shore of marsh grass at the cove.

"There it is!" shouted Rob, and high-stepped the lily pads into a zone of yellow-green water. Tony splashed after him, amazed that the evidence was so easily come by.

"Must be an underground stream to get here so quickly," Rob said. "No wonder the marsh is dying. With all that stuff the Mayor feeds his lawn and the speed with which it gets here, it's a wonder this place isn't a jungle." He asked if Tony thought the Mayor could be persuaded to stop fertilizing. Tony thought he might. "He likes frogs and votes." He thought a moment.

"Would fertilizer explain the disappearance of frogs?"

"Not unless the weeds grow in the fertilizer for so many years that the marsh becomes dry land.

"We've solved only *one* problem. That the Mayor is killing the marsh. As far as the death of Cock Robin is concerned, Mayor Joe is guiltless . . . so far." Rob took a test card out of his shirt pocket, explained it was for 2,4,5–T, the weed killer, and held it in the water. Tony sloshed over to him and watched eagerly. After minutes had passed they stood up and smiled at each other.

"Negative," said Tony.

When they got back to Tony's gate Rob said he figured they had found one clue in the Cock Robin mystery—a possible source of PCB, the dump.

"Now to find out where the boxes of stuff came from."

"Don't you know?" Tony asked in surprise.

"No. Where?"

"The Missatonic Mill. The name was stamped on those drums."

"What drums? There weren't any near me."

Tony reached into his pocket, took out the piece of yellow fabric he had found at the dump, and pointed to the burned edges.

"I found it in a blackened drum near the top of the heap."

Rob turned it over. "Where have I heard of this before?"

"On 'Cock Robin Hour.' The Mayor told about Mrs. R. decorating her nest with it." He reached for his notebook and then handed Rob the piece he found in the hedge.

"Wow!" Rob exclaimed. "This puts us close to solving the death of the eggs. PCB affects the shells; makes them very thin. Because of this some break, others dry out. The embryos in eggs three, four, and five in Cock Robin's nest were dessicated—lost too much water. They died before hatching. Lamberty is responsible for *that*, and . . . I don't like to speculate . . . but possibly the missing frogs." PCB, he reminded Tony, only came out of the atmosphere in the presence of rain or water. "Since frogs are wet-skinned, they must have absorbed a lethal dose," he surmised.

"I'm going to run a test on some lab frogs tomorrow," Rob said as they walked back to the road. Quickly he got on his bike explaining he wanted to get the tape to Craig and Dr. Melvin so they could analyze it and the yellow fabric. "We know what we're looking for, so it won't take long. Want to come with me?"

Tony did want to go to the lab and watch the mystery unfold in flasks and under microscopes, but said his time would be better spent breaking the news to Mary Alice. Rob agreed, asked Tony to call the Mayor and make an appointment around three o'clock for himself, Craig, and Dr. Melvin to discuss the report. He suggested Tony also ask Mr. Lamberty and tell the Mayor to put the fire out.

"We may know who killed Cock Robin. I'm going to find out what a lethal dose of PCB is and compare it with C.R.'s dose." He told Tony to bury his dump clothes and sped off.

6. The Flight

As Tony walked into the house he remembered his mother was holding breakfast.

"Sorry," he said as he came into the kitchen.

"Where's Rob?" she asked.

"He had to get to the lab." She looked so disappointed, he promised to ask him for dinner.

"What are you two up to? You act like a couple of Sherlock Holmeses."

Tony chuckled, swung his leg over the chair, and sat down. His mother put her hands on her hips. "This whole Cock Robin thing is getting all out of proportion," she said. "I mean like last night. The fight and the accusations. So a robin dies . . . I think the whole town's gone crazy, and you, too. Now get out there and help your pop rake the lawn."

"I'm afraid to," Tony smiled. "I might uncover some weed killer he's been using."

She took the pan of muffins out of the oven and placed them on the table. "I'm so tired of this whole pollution thing that I just might hop in the car and leave the engine running."

"Come on, Mom, you're sore because you couldn't feed Rob."

She tossed her head and smiled. "By the way, Mary Alice has called you twice."

Tony grabbed two muffins, gulped a glass of milk, and hurried out the back door. His father called him to come help. He shouted that he would be right back, cut through Mrs. Korkner's yard, and jogged down an alley to Maple Street. He jumped the sun blotches on the walk under the maples, then sprinted to the path that led to the Lamberty house, a mid-Victorian masterpiece of gingerbread and wooden towers. Mary Alice was on the far end of her vast front porch.

"How's Saddle?" he asked as he walked up the steps.

"He can fly!" she exclaimed. "And he follows me everywhere. I can't make a move that he's not right beside me."

"He's imprinted on you."

"What's that mean?"

"Well, he thinks you're his mother." Tony explained that when birds hatched from eggs, the first moving thing they saw, whether it was a person or a bird, was a "parent," particularly if food was associated with the moving object. He told her about a gosling in a University of Michigan experiment that followed a box that moved along a wire pully. The box occasionally dropped food and hence was a mother to the gosling. "You're 'mother' in Saddle's brain; and wherever you go, he goes."

Saddle had hopped from a rocker to the railing to Mary Alice's shoulder. Upon seeing Tony, he screamed and flew all the way down the porch. Mary Alice picked him up and brought him back. "Wow," Tony said, "ever since I grabbed him in the street, I've become his enemy. You may be Mama, but I'm sure not Papa. I'm the bad guy."

Mary Alice stroked Saddle, he looked up at her, and fluffed slightly, expressing his contentment.

"Tell me more about birds," she said.

"First, let me tell you about people." Tony plunked himself down on the steps, Mary Alice lowered herself slowly and sat rigidly beside him. Quickly he repeated Rob's story about PCB, then related the events at the dump. When he described the drums and yellow cloth, she tapped her fingers on the porch and pushed back that recalcitrant lock of hair.

"Are you going to tell me the cloth came from the mill?" Her fingers tightened on the edge of the porch.

"Yes."

She stared at him, eyes round and wide.

"But Daddy wouldn't burn anything there! He suggested the no-burn ordinance to the Mayor."

"Well, maybe the fire got started by spontaneous combustion. There's a lot of greasy junk out there."

"Oh, Tony, this is terrible!" She pushed back her hair again and held Saddle close to her cheek. He blinked, pecked softly at her ear, and shook.

"Tony, I've been accusing everyone else!" She looked down at her toes as her shoulders drooped and her chin quivered ever so slightly. "Did Daddy really kill Cock Robin?" she asked. Her hair tumbled over her face, but she did not push it back this time. "I feel awful."

"We still don't know what a lethal dose of PCB is, or if he got one. Also he got some DDT from somewhere, as well as lead and mercury. Not much of any. Perhaps they didn't even kill him."

"Daddy must not have known the fabric was dangerous," she went on as if he had not spoken.

"Mary Alice, remember when you were on the radio? You said something about birds dying in Florida."

"I remember."

"Where did you hear that?"

"Grandmother sent me a clipping. I'll get it." She jumped to her feet. "Why?"

"Maybe Cock Robin got something down there."

"In Florida?"

"Robins fly south, you know."

"Oh, Tony, you're just being nice. But I hope you're right." She put Saddle on the porch railing, ran into the house and up the steps. Tony could hear the sound of her footsteps fading down a long corridor in the rear of the house. Saddle flew to the door, then cocked his eye at Tony. Pressing his feathers to his body, stretching his neck, he assumed the pose of an alarmed bird that has seen an enemy. Tony knew all too well that he was that enemy, and tried to move away. Saddle screamed and winged professionally into the spruce tree. Clicking like a young juvenile rather than the fluttering baby he was when Mary Alice was present, he hopped from one limb up to the next until he was about thirty feet above the ground. When Mary Alice returned, Saddle was peering through the limbs and stretching his neck as he studied the sky.

"Sorry," said Tony, pointing to Saddle, "but I do scare him."

He jumped to the railing and started to climb the tree. "No, Tony," she said. "Let him go! Let him go! Then the Mayor can announce that Saddle is free in the clean Saddleboro air, and we can all forget the whole thing."

Tony took a grip on a limb and placed his foot on another. "Not until we put a band on him. We've got to mark that bird so that the people of Saddleboro will see and believe. Also, with a band on him, we might find out if he migrates to Florida. Someone just might find him."

Tony climbed swiftly up the tree, but just as he was about to catch him, Saddle took off and winged to the birch in the next yard. Scrambling down, he jumped over the porch railing and started up the birch. Mary

Alice arrived just as Saddle sailed on, flew all the way up Maple, and alighted on the corner curb. An auto horn scared him and he flew to a limb of an elm on the Commons. Twenty feet off the ground, he screamed in alarm as Tony darted across the street.

"Saddle, come here! Saddle, Saddle!" Mary Alice called. Don Curcio, the postmaster's son, who was mowing the grass, stopped his work and stared up at the bird.

"So that's our hero," he said, then looked across the street. "Hey, Ginger, come here. Look at Saddle! He's flying in the clean air of Saddleboro."

Ginger Pierce ran to the elm, followed by a little girl and two boys who were shouting: "There's Saddle! Look at Saddle!" The rush was on. Twenty to fifty people came out of the stores. Cars pulled up and stopped as people gathered under the elm. The postmaster, hearing the commotion, dashed into the street, saw John Pierce in his store, and called loudly, "Come see Saddle!"

Mrs. Korkner heard him from inside the drugstore, poked her head out, saw Saddle, and hurried to join the crowd.

"If everyone would go away," Mary Alice cried, "he'd come down."

"Why should he come down?" someone asked. "He's free in the Saddleboro air. The Mayor can wear his hat again."

"Yeah! Call the Mayor and tell him to put on his hat and come to the Commons."

"Please, please go away!" Mary Alice's voice was drowned by cheers for the Mayor. Tony stood beneath Saddle, head back, wondering what he should do.

"He's lovely," he heard Mrs. Korkner say.

Sergeant Sears arrived, eased his squad car through the crowd on the street, and joined Tony. Legs apart, arms folded, the policeman grinned up at the bird. Then fingernails dug into his arm and he looked down to see Mary Alice.

"Get the fire truck," she snapped. "Get the fire ladder. We must put a band on him before he goes."

"What?" Sergeant Sears pushed back his cap. "A band? What's he—a girl? No Cock Robin Junior of Saddleboro is going to wear a band as long as I'm in charge."

"Well, you aren't," Mary Alice said. "Science is in charge. He must be banded so we can study him." Sergeant Sears was not moved. "I know what a band is." He looked up again. "I also know that no one is going to find one banding record. It takes hundreds. I'm a duck hunter and I've only found two in my lifetime, and thousands of ducks are banded each year."

"But you found two. Please, call for the hook and ladder."

"Can't. It just went to the dump."

Mary Alice grew pale. "Why?" she asked.

"The Mayor ordered it. Some durn fool lit the dump, and noxious chemicals are burning. He says they're polluting the air."

Mary Alice stared at Tony, started to run home, then turned back to her bird.

"Tony, what'll I do?"

"Let's go fishing."

"Fishing?" she shrieked.

"I know where there's duckweed in the Missatonic. Where there's duckweed, there're fish."

"I don't know how to fish."

"Well, then, you can admire the tiniest flowering plant in the world—the duckweed."

"Tony Isidoro, you're impossible. It was your idea to band him."

Tony looked up as Saddle flexed his legs, lowered his wings, and pointed his beak toward the end of the Commons as he mapped out a course of flight. Tony grabbed Mary Alice by the arm and maneuvered her around Sergeant Sears and into the street.

"Saddle's headed for the Town Hall. Let's go." The young robin took off from the elm, sailed over their heads, and alighted between two Doric columns on the top of the steps. Everyone ran toward him cheering.

"He's healthier than I am," John Pierce said to the postmaster.

"He's going to give a speech!" a little girl shouted. "Yeah, he is," a boy agreed.

"Speech! Speech!" Ginger yelled.

Somehow, Mrs. Korkner arrived at the bottom of the Town Hall steps before anyone else and, lifting her fists, shook them at the oncoming crowd.

"Stupids!" she shouted. "Stop! You're scaring Saddle." Tony halted and Mary Alice crashed into him. The crowd behind slowed down and stopped.

"Now, everyone just turn around and go about your business," Mrs. Korkner ordered. "Saddle is free, and that's that!" Sweeping her palms like two frayed brooms, she came down the steps ordering the crowd back to the fountain. They obliged quietly; a few kids sat down on the lawn, and others followed their example. When almost everyone was seated, Saddle hopped along the porch, flew to the railing, preened, and sat down on his heels. A murmur went through the crowd, for Saddle was resting, and they could see his speckled breast, his folded wings, and shining eyes.

"I believe he's going to sleep," Sergeant Sears said to Tony.

"No," he corrected. "He's heard something. He's acting like a baby robin that's been given a signal to sit." Tony concentrated on a sound near the library.

"The miracle of Saddleboro is about to begin," he whispered excitedly to Mary Alice.

"Now what?" she asked with a lift to her voice.

"He's going to get parents right before our eyes. I heard a robin clink by the library. So did Saddle. That's why he's looking like a baby. How's his feed call? Can he give it now?"

"No. He can only scream at *you*."

Saddle cocked his head, stood up, and flattened his feathers to his body. Another clink sounded and he flew to the dogwood by the library, alighted, and fluttered his wings.

"He can beg. That's just as good," Tony said. "If the adults see that, they'll feed him."

"That's what he does to me when he's hungry—flutters."

"Begs," Tony corrected. "And that's good news. He'll get fed."

The spectators sensed something was about to happen and got to their feet. Sergeant Sears folded his arms on his chest, spotted the female near the top of the dogwood, and leaned over to Tony.

"Is this going to be a territorial fight?"

"No, foster parents."

Saddle fluttered again and opened his mouth. Down through the limbs dropped the female with food in her bill. She alighted near Saddle. He sidled up to her and opened his mouth. She stuffed it with food and flew off. The audience cheered.

"Shush!" Tony demanded. "Or he won't hear the signals from his new parents."

Saddle begged again, the female returned with more food; he ate and hopped close against the trunk of the tree. Shaking his feathers, he settled down on his heels to roost, an action that tightened the tendons in his back toes and clamped him to the limb so he would not fall as he napped. Suddenly he stood up. His eyes widened and his neck stretched up. Tony strained his ears, squeezed Mary Alice's arm, and smiled.

"Hear it?"

"No."

"The 'tut-tut'? Listen. He's being told to hide."

Saddle heard if Mary Alice did not. He spread his wings, flew into the rhododendron beside the library porch, and disappeared among the shiny leaves.

"That's it!" shouted Sergeant Sears. "Everybody go home and clean up your environment. Saddle has parents. All's well in Saddleboro." He took off his cap and shooed the onlookers toward the drugstore. Mrs. Korkner assisted until the crowd had thinned out and the Commons was speckled only with the bench sitters who sit in the sun every pleasant Saturday afternoon.

"Let's go fishing," Tony said to Mary Alice.

She tossed her head and stared at him icily.

"Now what?" Tony asked. "We've proved to everyone that Saddle is free. Are you mad because he isn't banded? The Sergeant is right; one doesn't help much. You need hundreds to get a single return." She did not answer and Tony tried another tactic. "I'm sorry I scared him—but it's a nice ending." He walked off whistling to himself. She followed reluctantly, but nevertheless followed, hesitating at the corner and dragging her feet down Elm. He walked slower and she caught up with him.

"I don't mean that!" she said. "I mean Daddy and the dump. Did you hear what the Sergeant said about the fire engines?"

"So?" Mary Alice saw her father's car parked in

front of the Mayor's house. She stopped and stared at it momentarily, then her eyes widened as if something had just occurred to her. Snapping her fingers, she hurried through Tony's gate and into the house.

"I don't have a rod."

"I'll lend you one."

While Tony was threading a line through the eyelets of a casting rod, the telephone rang. He answered it.

"Tone." It was Rob. "I'm at the Mayor's. Can't talk much. The PCB came from the stuff that was burning at the dump. All sources check: tape, yellow fabric, the cards from the marsh and river. But there was *not* enough in Cock Robin to kill him even with the DDT. So we're off again. The Mayor *does* fertilize heavily and we've got him for killing the marsh. I was going to accuse him of Saddle's deformity because I thought he *must* use a weed killer. But he doesn't. Sam digs the weeds up. So the 2,4,5–T comes from another source. Someone is using a lot of it despite the governmental ban. That soil sample I took by the hawk woods was saturated. Mrs. Robin could have eaten worms there and gotten the dose that affected Saddle's voice. As for Cock Robin, his death may be due to the mercury. There's more in him than we thought. That's Craig's field—hard metals—and he needs to find the source. Look over Izzy's maps and see if there's anything upriver—a factory, golf course. Call me back."

"How are things going?"

"Extraordinarily well."

Tony put down the phone and spun on his heel.

"Mary Alice!" he shouted. "Your dad didn't kill Cock Robin! There wasn't enough PCB in him to be fatal!" She stood very still and stared out the window.

Tony waited for her to say something, but she did not, so he bounded up the stairs to Izzy's room and took out the Saddleboro County map. Beyond the college the highway left the river and wound across a mountain to Kent, but the town was not on the Missatonic watershed, so Tony ignored it and studied the land near the river. From Saddleboro to the mountain were farms. No help. He was about to go downstairs when he noticed that Izzy had printed on one side of Turkey Hill the word "Pine Plantation." Tony had gone hiking there last summer and couldn't remember it. He looked closer. A stream called Twig's Run came down through the plantation and emptied into the Missatonic. Since he had not gone all the way down the road, he had no knowledge of the stream. He went back to the kitchen and called Rob.

"There's nothing upstream like a factory or golf course," he said. "Just farms way back from the water. The river bank's steep along there and the farmers have left it in trees."

"Hmm."

"There is *one* odd thing. Izzy has a pine plantation marked on Turkey Hill. I was up there last summer and it was all open land."

"Open? Like what's growing there?"

"Weeds . . . a few little evergreens."

"Replantings, do you think?" Rob sounded excited and suggested they meet tomorrow early and have a look. He hung up. Tony reported the news to Mary Alice, but she was not particularly delighted to hear they were looking for a source of mercury.

"I thought you'd be happy to know there's another villain."

"I'm not."

"Oh, stop feeling so guilty."

"It's just that the Lambertys have a name in Saddleboro and Daddy cares about the people in this town. I can't imagine his burning a noxious product!"

"Maybe he didn't know."

"He knew. He's a chemist. Our mill was the first in New England to make synthetic fabrics . . . and *he* helped develop them. He keeps tabs on every synthetic made at the mill."

Tony handed her an apple, picked up the rods and his tackle box in one hand, and opened the door with the other. They walked down Maple to the Missatonic without speaking. At the river's edge Tony proudly pointed to the little patches of duckweed he had found.

"There's not much but they mean the sewage-disposal plant *is* helping Saddleboro and the wildlife." Mary Alice replied that everyone knew *that*, including her father, who was paying for most of it in higher taxes.

The Flight

Tony had not meant to start an argument. He waded into the water and looked for insect larvae for bait, pausing about three feet out, for he could see the bottom for the first time in his life. Circles of sunlight moved across stones and a snail plowed its silent course. He wanted to tell Mary Alice, but thought better of it, waded ashore, and baited her hook.

7. The Mill

Mary Alice slammed her rod over her head, the reel sang, the line zigzagged, and the bait splashed on the water. "I've got a bite!" she screamed, yanked, and pulled out a fish. It shot across Tony's shoulder, off the hook, and into the woods. He leaped over a picnic table and picked it up.

"Carp," he said as he showed it to her. "Know what it means?"

"That I caught a fish and you didn't." She was feeling better, Tony observed, as he crossed his feet and let himself down to a sitting position. With a sigh he put his elbows on his knees, his chin in his fists, and stared across the water.

"It means—I'll tell you a natural history story—

"Many years ago the Missatonic was a trout stream—

the most beautiful kind of waterway in the world. Clear, icy water sparkled over rocks and stones and in this water kingdom the brook trout was king. His dukes were sticklebacks, mud minnows, and sand shiners, and they all lived together in a nation of shady cold water that never got to seventy degrees. Then came the farmers. They cut down trees to the river's edge. Sunlight fell on the water and it warmed. Because it warmed it couldn't hold as much oxygen and the king trout died. He was replaced by the bass king, which doesn't need so much oxygen. His dukes were the bluegills and black crappies. The Missatonic had changed, even the snails and plants were different. Next came the industrial revolution and pollution. The bass king was replaced by the carp."

"Carp are fun to catch." She cast again and Tony stretched out on his back.

A quiet half hour passed without another bite.

"Let's go down the river," Mary Alice suggested. "Maybe the fishing's better there."

They crossed the foot of Town Park, walked the rail fence at the end of Maple Street, and jumped into the parking lot of the Missatonic Mill. Mary Alice looked up at the building, commented on the rosy color of the brick walls, and said they were almost two hundred years old.

"These bricks mark the beginning of the industrial revolution in America."

She climbed to the retaining wall along the river.

117.

Tony leaped up beside her and peered down. The water moved slowly behind the dam, then broke into a ragged waterfall and splashed for a few hundred yards before slowing down again.

"The old mill got its power from those falls," Mary Alice said. "A waterwheel turned the first mechanical spinning jenny. It's called the 'mule.' It could make many fine threads at one time. Spinning wheels made but one. We still have it. Want to see it?"

"Sure."

Tony watched the water spill through the breaks in the unrepaired dam and noted the mud behind it. The dam had also contributed to the passing of the trout, for as it slowed the water, the silt dropped out and covered the stones the trout laid their eggs on. He cast his line and was watching the circles it made when Mary Alice jumped down from the wall and called to him to come see the mill. He suspected he was going to get the other side of his trout story. He joined her.

As they walked toward the mill Tony learned that the first Lamberty to come to America from England was a carpenter. He did well and sent his son Will to college in London. Will did not study. He spent most of his time with two young men who had an idea called a factory. They built a large building, put ten water-powered looms in it, and hired people to do nothing but weave. They bought raw materials in large quantities, paid less for them, and sold the yardgoods more cheaply than the people who wove by hand. Will, seeing them grow rich on this idea, came back to Saddleboro and built the Missatonic Mill.

Mary Alice rambled on about Will's son, who made a fortune during the Civil War producing twill for Union Army uniforms, and his son who did very well after the Civil War. Then she stopped talking and Tony realized she had walked him to the other side of the mill where the new tank truck was parked.

When he had commented properly on it she went to the office door, turned the knob, and found it locked. "That's odd," she said as she opened a panel in the woodwork and pushed an emergency button.

While they waited she chatted on about her grand-father and how during his life the mill became famous for fine rugs. He used natural dyes from plants that two Indian women who lived in town gathered in the forests. "Subtle greens, golds, and browns," she said. "The rich reds and blues came from madder and indigo plants that were grown in a garden where this parking lot is."

Tony nodded and Mary Alice asked him if he wanted to see one of the rugs. "They are jewels, but Granddad switched to aniline dyes after World War II and stopped making rugs because nobody wanted them. Today it's different. People are beginning to appreciate those things again. Dad would make the rugs again if he could find the wild plants; but their names were lost when the Indian women passed away.

"Want to see where they were made?"

Tony *was* curious about this, for those rugs were his

family's one connection with the Missatonic Mill. Mrs. Isidoro's father had been brought over from Italy to cultivate madder and indigo.

There was no response to the bell, so Mary Alice pounded on the door. Several minutes passed, a key turned, and an elderly watchman appeared.

"Miss Lamberty," he said. "Come in. Sorry to be so long."

Mary Alice looked around suspiciously, then walked across the reception room.

"Come see Daddy's office," she said to Tony. "He redid the room where the old waterwheel machinery was housed." Tony was game, although the mill was dark and he really preferred to be outdoors.

Hand-hewn beams framed the room and the waters of the Missatonic splashed down a wall of glass. The office was beautiful: sunlight shone through the water and cast moving shadows around the room.

"Dad's really a nature lover at heart," she said, tracing the path of a bubble's reflection down the wall.

Tony sat down in a leather chair, stretched out his feet, and pointing to an odd contraption in the corner, asked her what it was.

"The first spinning jenny in America." She smiled. "That's the mule I was telling you about."

"Would you like to see the rug of natural dyes?" He really wanted to and followed her down a narrow corridor to a solid wooden door that must have come from a tree the size of which Tony would never behold. She opened it, switched on a light, and led him up a narrow staircase to a paneled room that no varnish had ever touched. It glowed with the patina of time. Three hand looms with intricately patterned rugs in various stages of completion stood before him.

"Dad lets women from the Weavers Club work here. He's sending one of them to the Rhode Island School of Design because she's so talented.

"The women do nice work, but they use aniline dyes and they're so garish." She opened a closet, pulled down a rug, and unrolled it on the floor. Tony gazed at colors that glowed like an autumn forest. Even *he* knew the rug was unusual.

"See the difference? Isn't this rich?" Tony could only nod and stare at the colors. For the first time in his life he felt the presence of the grandfather his mother so often told him about. It was an odd sensation.

"Where are the modern looms?" he asked, as he helped Mary Alice put the rug back.

She led him through another door to a catwalk above the main loom room. Huge machines and wheels linked with belts stood below them.

"There's even a computer to tell those monsters what designs to weave," Mary Alice said, but Tony really was more interested in fishing. He noticed the exit at the bottom of a circular staircase and hurried toward it. As he was about to lunge down the steps Mary Alice opened another door and Tony was looking into a laboratory of flasks, vats, bottles, and instruments. Two men leaned over a table of papers. One wore the uniform of an Air Force colonel.

"Oh, excuse me," Mary Alice said politely. The civilian turned around and Tony recognized Wally, the foreman. "My friend and I were out fishing," she went on, "and since he's never seen the mill, I'm showing him around." She walked up to the Colonel and extended her hand.

"I'm Mary Alice Lamberty. My father owns the mill." Wally said "Hi" to her and turned back to the papers.

"Fishing?" the Colonel said pleasantly. "Any luck?"

"A carp." Mary Alice answered. The officer smiled, then leaned over the papers.

"Let's go," Tony said, but Mary Alice did not budge, she kept staring at the Colonel. Tony could not figure what she was up to. She looked as if she were getting up her nerve to dive headfirst off a high diving board. He tugged her sleeve and she advanced one step toward the Colonel.

"Daddy told me this morning that you were coming," she blurted. "But he didn't tell me why and he didn't tell me that he had been burning a noxious chemical at the dump. It's been contaminating our town, and killing birds and things."

"So?"

"Well, it occurred to me that you might have something to do with it . . ." her voice trembled, "the burning, I mean."

The Colonel frowned, but Tony at last understood why Mary Alice had brought him to the mill. She wanted to find out for herself if her father had started the fire. Now he could help her. He stepped forward and told the Colonel not only the story of Cock Robin but about the research that was being conducted on the Saddleboro environment.

"Mr. Lamberty has violated the no-burn ordinance of the township," he said, "and Mary Alice and I are wondering if someone else made the decision."

"Oh, that?" said the Colonel. "Well, yes. I'm with NASA, the Space Administration. Mr. Lamberty has been making a special fabric for space flight and it ran into some problems in the final test. Since its components are a military secret, NASA wanted the batches destroyed. We *ordered* your father to burn them, Mary Alice."

"Didn't anyone know the cloth contained PCB?" Tony asked. The Colonel wanted to know what *that* was and Tony explained. He elaborated on its effects on wildlife. The Colonel replied that he doubted if anyone in Washington had tested it for its effects on birds, but thought they should have.

"Well, I agree," Mary Alice said, her sparkiness returning. "Someone down there in Washington should think of these things. You've gotten my father in a terrible position."

"I'm only following orders," the Colonel said. "I'm here today because I must see to it that one more lot is burned." He sat down on the edge of the table. "But I'm also concerned about our air and streams. I'm a fisherman myself."

"Well, then," Mary Alice said promptly, "you won't burn the last batch, will you?"

"What do you suggest?"

"Burying it in wet cement," Tony answered.

"Will that prevent pollution?"

"It's better than burning."

The Colonel pondered a moment. "Is your father at home, Mary Alice?" She told him he was at a meeting at the Mayor's but could be reached. She was about to dial him when the phone rang. It was her father and he wanted to speak to the Colonel. Mary Alice handed him the receiver and he talked a few minutes, hung up, and ran his hand through his hair.

"Well, you kids are right. This is a mess; but your dad's in touch with my office in Washington and they, too, are concerned about the situation. They're going to call me and change the orders." He smiled at Mary Alice. "Does that make you feel better?"

"Well, of course. Doesn't it make you feel better?"

The phone rang again; the Colonel answered it, spoke a few words, then looked at Tony. "You can go back to your fishing," he said. "We're clearing the details on how to bury the fabric in wet cement." He winked. "Good luck."

Tony grinned like a crocodile, ran out the door and down the steps. Mary Alice was close behind when he opened the exit door and burst into the sunlight.

"NASA polluted Saddleboro!" she shouted gleefully and ran to the retaining wall, scrambled onto it, skipped to the end, and jumped into the parking lot. When Tony caught up her eyes were filled with tears.

"Why are you crying? Aren't you glad?"

"I doubted him." She sobbed. "I doubted him."

"No, you didn't. You've been defending him all day." When she kept on crying Tony picked up the fishing rods and walked off in despair. At the river he cast his line and forgot Mary Alice. A carp had grabbed his bait and was taking off for the other side of the river. When he landed the fish Mary Alice picked up her rod and dangled it in the water.

Tony cast again, whistled, and looked around. He saw a grove of maples across the river and remembered something, put down his rod, and walked upstream to the shallows. He crossed to the opposite shore and climbed the hill. After a brief search he found a lobe-leafed plant and carried it back to Mary Alice.

"This is a bloodroot plant," he said. "It makes a beautiful red dye. Mom uses it for wool hats and mittens. You add alum to the roots and boil them for about half an hour."

"Tony! Why didn't you tell me you knew dye

plants. Wait'll I tell Dad! Maybe we can make the rugs again!" She dropped her rod and dipped the plant in the water.

As Tony cast he told Mary Alice the woods was full of plants that were once used to dye wool and linen. "Mom knows them," he said. "My grandfather taught them to her. I'll ask her what they are." He watched his line drift into a deep pool.

"Who's your grandfather?" Mary Alice asked suspiciously.

"He was invited over from Italy by your grandfather to grow those madder and indigo plants."

Mary Alice's eyes sparkled. "You mean he was Giuseppe Violanti?"

Tony nodded, pleased that she knew his name, and squinted at the sun. He estimated that it was about quarter to five and that the conference would be over, his mother almost ready to serve dinner. He picked up the rods and tackle box.

"I'd better get you home," he said, and started up the hill.

8. Who Really Did Kill Cock Robin?

The meeting at the Mayor's house was still in progress when Tony came down Elm. He loitered a moment at the gate, looked at the sky, and decided he had time to bike the four miles to the pine plantation before dark. If the killer of Cock Robin was not DDT and PCB, perhaps it *was* the mercury. He went to the garage, took a map out of the car, and spread it on the ground. The road he had hiked on last summer near Izzy's "Pine Plantation" was not shown on the map. He wondered why, decided to look for himself, and wheeled his bike into the alley.

Beyond the college he left the highway and followed a macadam road for about half a mile, then turned off on the narrow dirt road he had walked last summer. He biked along this, recalling the big maples and beeches, even the rocks at the side of the road, until he came to the field where his hike had ended. As he studied the hill he saw why he had not remembered the plantation. The trees had been cut down. Stumps poked above young low weeds. But last summer the plants had been so tall they had covered the stumps and he had not realized that the hill had been logged.

That answered that, but in no way explained the mercury. There was not even a house, just stumps, seedlings, and weeds. He turned around to go home when he realized the road was new, about a year old. The rocks at the side were not weathered, but sharp and newly broken. Curious, he biked on. The sun was dipping behind Turkey Hill when he rounded a bend and came upon a new building. Beside it flowed what he surmised was Twig's Run. It was jammed with logs and Tony knew he had found a pulp mill, many of which were springing up in Saddleboro County. He tried to recall if Rob had said anything about pulp mills polluting the environment, thought not, and started home again when two men came out of the mill. One was a huge blond, the other looked like Tony's father, moustache and all. He hesitated to approach them, for his question about mercury seemed ridiculous in this natural environment.

The big blond man shouted, "Whatdayawant?" Tony felt awkward, looked at his feet, and saw the label of a chemical company on a battered crate. His courage returned. Eagerly he ran over to the men, explained he was working for Mayor Joe Dambrowski, and asked if the mill used a mercury product for any purpose. "Joe Dambrowski!" the huge man expostulated. "The conservationist who killed Cock Robin wants to know *that?*"

Tony felt embarrassed, then he thought of Rob, Craig, Dr. Melvin, and Mr. Lamberty and he gathered his courage to persist.

"Well, do you?"

"Sure we use mercuric oxide. It takes the slime off logs that sit in the water too long. That answer your question?" He chuckled.

Tony's heart thumped. Had he found the killer of Cock Robin, the final arrow that had sent the polluted bird to its death?

Excitedly he jumped on his bike, remembered he would have to prove this claim, and rushed to the dump to find a bottle in which to collect water from Twig's Run.

The blond man shouted that the area was closed and that he had better get out. Tony hestitated, then tore the label off the crate, hoping it would be of some help to Rob.

As he wheeled down the road he heard the men's car start. They passed him slowly and for the next hundred feet, Tony could see the big blond watching him in the rear-view mirror. Then he accelerated the car, rounded the bend, and disappeared. Tony felt like a real detective.

When he arrived home Rob was in the kitchen talking to his mother as she sliced mushrooms.

"Tone!" she exclaimed as he tossed his coat in the closet. "Rob's got a job. The Mayor's asked him to be his Conservation Aide. Isn't that splendid? Little Rob who used to go fishing with my Izzy."

"Yeah, Tone, it's just what I've been looking for," Rob said. "An opportunity to pin down environmental problems, talk them over with the people at Town Hall meetings, and advise lawmakers like the Mayor. From now on we scientists are going to have to assume our responsibility to the Earth. We made the problem, we're going to have to solve it."

Tony was sorry to hear that a good scientist like Rob would take a political job.

"You think that's more important than research?" he asked.

"For the next two thousand years, yes!" Rob crossed his feet and leaned back in his chair. "By the way, the Mayor doesn't want you to resign. Says you're the best detective he's had on his staff. What'll you be doing after school next year?"

Tony felt his ears grow warm and slid down in his chair. He was glad to be wanted but embarrassed that he had not finished his job. He avoided answering by asking Rob a question.

"Will you still do research?"

"Sure." Rob looked at him. "Don't you want to know who killed Cock Robin?"

"Yes!" Tony sat up. "Who did?"

"Well, here we go again. It's another long story." He began by saying that Craig had found the DDT users. One of the chemical companies he had written had delivered a large quantity of DDT to apple growers twenty miles to the northwest. Ordinarily their sprays did not reach Saddleboro, the damp springs bringing it to earth in their own valley. However, this year had been dry and the DDT had drifted southeast on the prevailing winds right into the still air above the valley where Saddleboro lay. It settled to earth in alarming amounts. Leaves, grass, everything was coated. The dose particularly affected the larvae of the cabbage looper, which had been weakened by a parasite, and this nestling food was all but wiped out—except in a few places, the Mayor's well-washed yard being one. His loopers were only lightly contaminated, survived, and passed on the small amounts they had eaten to Cock Robin.

"Fortunately he was a first-year bird, I could tell by his tissues, therefore he didn't have as much DDT in him as an older bird would have gathered in his travels to and from the south. So he didn't die.

"Next Lamberty began burning the yellow fabric in early May. The stuff smolders slowly, it doesn't burst into flame, and so for weeks it drifted into Saddleboro on those same prevailing winds and was locked over the valley. It combined with the dew and shellacked the plants. Once again the PCB did not harm Cock Robin; but Mrs. Robin was different. She apparently was older *and* she accumulated the chemical during the egg-laying period. Each eggshell was thinner than the one before it. Saddle must have been the first she laid. He made it.

"Mrs. Robin then picked up 2,4,5–T, the weed killer, from an as yet unknown source. This chemical, as you know, affects the behavior and normality of offspring. The songless Saddle, the one that lived, is a victim of this chemical.

"We'll never know what killed Mrs. Robin because we can't test her, but apparently it was three years of pollution. If Cock Robin had been three years old, or even two, at the rate he was storing DDT and PCB, he would have died from those chemicals too."

Tony wanted to know if Rob had tested the frogs with PCB and he replied that he had. Three out of ten were dead and the rest couldn't hop or croak.

Rob also thought the combination of chemicals had either driven off or even killed the marsh hawks. They were old enough to have stored an abundance of chemicals in their bodies. He and Izzy had banded the female four years ago.

"Wow!" Tony put his hands on his head. "Let's see now. The Mayor killed the marsh; Lamberty killed the eggs and maybe Mrs. Robin; 2,4,5–T from an unknown source deformed Saddle. Anything else?"

"Yes," Rob said. "Who Really Killed Cock Robin?"

"When do we eat, Mom? I need food!" Tony said in despair.

Mrs. Isidoro answered his question by placing a

caldron of minestrone soup in the middle of the table and serving three piping hot bowls.

"Pa will be late—as usual," she said, and went right on to tell Rob he looked thin and gaunt and asked when he was going to get married. Obviously he could not feed himself properly, no man could, she thought. Rob told her he still could not find a girl who could cook like she did. She beamed happily and served him more soup.

Rob turned to Tony and said the mercury in Cock Robin was still perplexing Craig, and Tony said he had checked upriver and found a pulp mill that was using it. He rummaged in his pocket, found the label, and put it victoriously on the table.

"Great!" Rob said, "but if you're thinking the pulp mill killed our friend, it didn't. Craig and Dr. Melvin were misled. After listening to the 'Cock Robin Hour' they assumed the Mayor's yard was along the river because Lowenthal, who's a pretty good naturalist when he has time, said the bird bathed there. They had found mercury on the river bottom and wanted you to check its source. Of course Cock Robin didn't get it from the river but somehow he did get mercury."

Rob put the label in his wallet and told Tony it was the first place he would visit on his new job. Mercury from pulp and paper mills had apparently been the major killer of Lake Erie. Its bottom was now good only for making thermometers.

"As for Cock Robin," Rob said when he had finished his soup, "we've tracked down everything now, *but* the final disaster that killed him. He had enough pollutants in him that one more thing would have done it. What was it? Frankly, I'm back to your outbreak of ants and bees."

Tony jumped up. "Come upstairs!" His mother had taken away the soup bowls and was poking the *pollo al diavolo,* broiled deviled chicken, with a fork. The main course was not quite ready to be served and Tony took Rob to his room.

As he took the glass top off his terrarium he reminded Rob that he had caught a pair of spiders the last time they were at the ant outbreak near the hawk woods. Rob looked at them. The female sat on her web eating a fruit fly, the male hunched on a leaf across from her.

"They look healthy. Is there something wrong?"

"They can't mate." They had been sitting in the same positions for four days, which is very unusual. Soon after a male ground spider spins its sperm web, the only web he builds, he drops sperm on it, then places his sex feet, or pedipalpi, in it and absorbs the life code. Come rain, storm, heat, or wind he then sets off to find a female, lasso her with webbing, and place his feet and sperm in a special pocket in her abdomen. This particular male had absorbed the sperm and then sat still.

"It was as if he were programmed wrong. I've been watching him for days. And I know he hasn't mated or she would have eggs by now."

"Sounds like we're back to Saddle's problem—2,4, 5–T and behavioral changes."

"Yeah," said Tony. "No baby spiders to grow up and eat ants would make for billions of ants, billions of bluettes, and billions of bees."

"Right," said Rob. "Now let's find out who's putting it there. Where did you say the outbreaks of ants and bees have occurred?"

"The Park, the field near the hawk woods, and the foreman's yard. These I'm sure of. There are probably more."

"Now, let's go to Izzy's map and see if they have anything in common." The map of "Human Habitations" was on the floor where Tony had left it. Rob went down to his hands and knees in one movement and Tony got down beside him. They looked at the ant-outbreak spots in silence.

"Power towers, but too far away to be significant," Rob said. Tony reached for a red pencil and drew circles around the ant areas. When he had them plotted they didn't make much sense, for each was in a slightly different spot from the other in relation to the towers; then he remembered how crazy the drainage under the Mayor's lawn had been and his first impression of the complexity of ecology when he had seen all of Izzy's maps. He reached for the weather and wind map; and there was the answer. Because of the terrain and houses, the prevailing winds came through Saddleboro erratically and Izzy's wind lines flowed over the spots where the ants were. He pointed this out to Rob.

"You've got it," Rob said. "You've got it. It *is* coming from the power towers. What on earth does electricity have to do with 2,4,5–T? It's a weed killer."

"Is anyone going to eat?" called Tony's mother. "Or shall I just feed this to Mrs. Korkner's cat?" Rob was downstairs almost before she finished her last sentence. He halted at the bottom. The table was a cornucopia. The crackling chicken was surrounded by a dish of baked tomatoes stuffed with anchovies, tuna, and black olives; another of braised sweet peppers and onions, and a plate of stuffed pasta tubes in tomato sauce. There was also a dish of lasagna, a basket of homemade bread, and a bowl of raw mushroom salad on the serving table.

"I'll never marry," Rob chided.

As Tony sat down he asked how the Mayor felt about killing the Saddleboro Marsh and Rob said he was very sorry about it. "I once thought he was all politics and corny phrases, but the death of Cock Robin really got to him. He called the Conservation Service immediately and asked them to help him keep his grass green without fertilizing the marsh.

"You know, when he did that, I knew I had been right to accept the job. People *will* stop polluting the earth when they see what they're doing. Oh, I don't mean that the Mayor is going to change. He'll still have his green grass; but he'll find another way to do it. And Lamberty will still make profits, but he'll find another way also. The Mayor and Lamberty are reeds. They are still small enough to bend. Government, industry, large organizations are perhaps dinosaurs. They can no longer adjust. The reeds must start a new environment."

"Rob, is the food all right."

"Mom, why didn't you have a daughter?"

Mr. Isidoro burst in the back door, apologizing for being late and explained as he took off his coat that an emergency had arisen at the sewage-disposal plant. "One of the filters broke down."

"Mayor Joe arrived as I was about to leave," he said. "He had a man from the Soil Conservation Service with him. Know what he suggested for the Mayor's lawn instead of fertilizers?" Tony and Rob looked up curiously. "First he told us about an experiment at the Pennsylvania State College where water is being piped from the sewage-disposal plant into a forest and sprayed over the trees. The nitrogens that aren't filtered out completely are useful there. Makes the trees grow like crazy. By the time the water seeps back to the stream it's pure.

"So he suggested to the Mayor that he do the same thing, pipe water from the plant to his lawn. Not only would he make use of the waste nitrogens, and be purifying the water as nature does, but he would have the greenest lawn in the state."

"I'll bet *that* pleased Mayor Joe," Rob said.

"Pleased him! He was fairly jumping. Said he was going home to call the Governor and tell him he could keep his state senate seat. He wants to stay right in

Saddleboro where he can pass some antipollution laws and become the expert on disposal water and green lawns." Rob smiled.

After dinner the Isidoros and Rob sat on the front porch talking about the old days when Izzy and Rob used to crawl out the window and down the rainspout to go fishing and collecting.

"And to think I knew nothing about it until Izzy told me before he went in the Army."

"What would you have done if you had known?" Tony asked.

"I'd have spanked him, big as he was."

"I don't blame you," said Rob. "Terrible thing we did."

Promptly at five A.M. Tony jumped from the rainspout to the ground. Rob was at the gate. Tony suggested they go to the Commons before starting out to see if Saddle were still being fed by the library robins. Rob agreed and they jogged off.

As they approached the fountain the male began his dawn song, a sleepy chirp that became a trill as he awakened. The air smelled of mown grass, and the streets looked so peaceful it was hard for Tony to believe that Saddleboro was polluted. He sat down on the Town Hall steps beside Rob and listened to the end of the dawn song of the male robin. A few songbirds joined him, but for the most part it was a solo to the changing Earth.

Suddenly Tony stood up and pointed down Pine Street. A Power and Light Company truck was moving toward the river. He and Rob took off at racing speed and met it on Crow Hill Road northwest of Wally's house. One of the two men had started up the tower, the other was inspecting the base. Tony said good morning and watched the ground man climb into the back of the truck. He asked him what was wrong and learned that a break in the line was cutting off power to the neighborhood. The man picked up a large sprayer, and, as calmly as possible, Tony asked him what it was used for.

"To keep down the weeds and trees, so's they won't interfere with the low lines that come into town."

"You spraying with 2,4,5–T?"

"Yeah."

Tony looked at Rob and Rob looked at him. Without further words they turned and ran back to the Commons. Rob slipped into the phone booth and dialed.

"Craig," he said, "Rob here. We may have a last clue. The Power and Light Company is using the 2,4,5–T." Apparently Craig had been asleep, for Rob apologized but wanted to know if Dr. Melvin had found any 2,4,5–T in Cock Robin.

Rob listened, asked a few more questions, then joined Tony on the lawn.

"No dice. None in Cock Robin. Only the eggs and consequently Mrs. R. Now how did she get it and not Cock Robin?"

"Same as the DDT and PCB. She's older and has been living in that yard for three years at least. I looked up Izzy's notes. I know she's the same bird because she's a kooky nest builder. One year she nested in a bucket, last year on a rake in the tool shed, this year in the Mayor's hat."

"And the Power and Light Company's been spraying for years!" Rob exclaimed. "She accumulated it. Well, now to educate the Power Company."

Tony looked across the Commons, caught a movement in an elm, and saw Saddle wing to the steps of the library.

He told Rob he was going to get Mary Alice and took off at a trot for Maple Street. The Lamberty house was quiet, no one was up, so he slipped around to the back of the house and studied the windows. He had really become a sleuth. He remembered she had run to the back of the house when she went to her room for the newspaper clipping. Observing that one window was trimmed with white ruffled curtains and opened halfway, he took a chance, picked up a pine cone and tossed it, missed and threw another. It went through the open window. Ready to accelerate to thirty miles an hour if Mr. Lamberty appeared, Tony waited, knees bent, feet aimed for Maple Street. A small figure moved behind the curtain, and to his relief Mary Alice, whom he had awakened with the cone, threw it out again. He put his fingers in his mouth and whistled.

"Oh," she said, popping her head out the window.

He beckoned to her, she withdrew, and he walked toward the front of the house to wait for her to dress and come downstairs. She arrived almost as soon as he. When he told her Saddle was on the library steps she sprinted up the street so fast he was forced to run hard to keep up with her. At the top of the hill he pointed to Saddle, who was fluttering his wings and acting like a baby robin.

"Should I catch him?" she asked. "Do you think he'll recognize me?"

Tony assured her he would. She started to run, then stopped.

"It's better this way," she said. "I'll leave him with his new mother."

"Go on and get him," Tony urged. "I have a colored band that we can put on his leg so we will know who he is for the rest of the spring and summer."

She walked slowly to the library and sat down on the steps. The male and female cried in alarm and dove at her head, but she did not move. Saddle hopped toward her, stopped, and cocked his eye at his new parents. Then he fluttered his wings and begged food from Mary Alice. She reached down and picked him up. Saddle balanced on her shoulder as she came back to the fountain.

Tony told her not to come too close, for if Saddle saw him he would take off for Florida.

"Put your hand around him and hold his wings firmly to his sides. Then turn him on his back and stroke his belly. This will hypnotize him so I can put on the band."

When Saddle was in a trance Tony told Mary Alice to take one foot between her thumb and forefinger and gently extend his leg. He then snapped the band on the tarsus and stepped back. Mary Alice walked to the library and placed him on the steps. Saddle stood up, shook his feathers, and after looking brightly around, flew into the dogwood tree. Mary Alice raced back to Tony and Rob.

"That's the best ending of all! Now everyone can recognize Saddle and remember to pick up trash and put filters on their cars!"

She wanted to know if Saddle would stay in the Commons where people could see him and Tony assured her he would; perhaps until August, when his foster parents were done with the breeding season. Their feelings about territory would then pass away and they would move around town. Finally they would gather with other robins in the fields and start south.

She sat down on the grass and hugged her knees.

"This is really nice, Tone," she said. "At least the Lambertys have done *one* good thing. We've saved Saddle. Because of him we may do some more good. Dad said if your mom could bring him the dye plants he would make those beautiful rugs again. He's tired of synthetics. Wants to make the Missatonic Mill the home of industrial ecology." She looked up at him. "He remembers your grandfather well."

Who Really Did Kill Cock Robin?

Rob was staring at his notebook and rubbing his beard. His long legs were stretched out on the grass and he looked more like a farmer than a scholar and politician.

"I think we're licked as far as Cock Robin's concerned," he said. "We've only got two villains, the apple growers who sprayed DDT and NASA. We still need to know who employed the killer mercury and *who* shot the final arrow into the polluted bird."

The telephone on the corner rang and Rob answered it. He came back grinning.

"Wow!" he said. "That helps."

Craig had just received a call from a friend in Washington, an assistant research director of the Wildlife Bureau. He had seen their report on Saddleboro and the unanswered source of the mercury. He told Craig that fungicides are full of the metal and that golf courses use them liberally to keep the grass from turning brown with fungi. Thousands of birds and fish are killed by golf courses. The man thought there might be one in Saddleboro.

When Craig told him no, the friend then suggested they check the seeds the farmers buy. Many are treated with mercurial compounds for the same reason—to kill fungi that attack and rot them.

"The Mayor!" exclaimed Mary Alice. "The Friends of Cock Robin saw a fungicide in his shed."

"That's right," Tony said. "You mentioned it in your letter-to-the-editor. There goes the Mayor's nice clean record. He did contribute to Cock Robin's death along with NASA and the orchard growers."

"Okay," said Rob. "He's the next one to educate."

"We're close," said Tony. "But still not there. Who done it?"

They stretched out on their backs and pondered in silence, and so they did not see Mayor Joe until he was almost upon them.

"Good morning," the Mayor said. All three sat up. He was wearing his Stetson hat!

"Saddle's not exactly flying in clean air," he said, "but he's flying!" He sat down on the grass beside them.

"Saddleboro has a real surprise in store for it. The Commons will soon be as green as my lawn . . . and without chemical fertilizers." He then went on to explain that Mrs. Korkner had given the town a gift, pipes to bring water from the disposal plant to the Commons, where the rich waste water would rise out of sprinklers, fall to the ground, and feed the grass.

Tony asked him if he were going to use fungicides.

"Why should I?" he asked. "This water is nature's best greener." Tony let the matter drop. Rob could tell him the bad news.

Mary Alice was fascinated to learn about Mrs. Korkner's gift and Rob was pleased, but Tony could not get enthusiastic. He still had not done his job. He had not found out who really killed Cock Robin. Everyone but he had done what he or she had set out to do.

Rob had isolated the chlorinated hydrocarbons, Craig the hard metals, and Mary Alice had raised Saddle. Even the Mayor had done his part. He had shifted from chemicals to the piped water. Only, he, Tony, had failed. He rolled over on his stomach and thumped the ground.

The Mayor, wearing the smile of self-satisfaction, crossed his legs and leaned back on his hands. He looked at the three. "Does this conference of nature detectives mean we have the criminal?"

"No!" snapped Tony. "All the pollutants together that were in Cock Robin were not enough to kill him. He shouldn't have died, that's all."

"QUIET!" They all turned to see David Lowenthal leaning out his apartment window above the *Patent Reader* office.

"It's Sunday, for goodness' sake. I want to sleep!"

"I have a news story for you!" the Mayor shouted. "A gift to Saddleboro. I want two cents a word!"

"I'll pay when I know who killed Cock Robin!" He pulled in his head.

A thin cry sounded in the distance. Tony and Rob jumped to their feet and looked west above the treetops, as flying high over the Post Office came the marsh hawk, its broad wings motionless as it rode a rising thermal current from the warming land.

"We've done something right!" Tony said with relief. "Marshy's back at the top of his pyramid."

"The fire's out! The fumes must have driven him off," Rob said. "They were pretty irritating, huh, Tone?"

"Quiet!" shouted Lowenthal once more.

Tony heard Mary Alice laugh at the sleepy editor, but did not look up. He was disgusted with himself. Picking a grass blade, he crushed it in his fingers and jabbed it into the ground.

"Dawn is beautiful," Mary Alice whispered. "All problems seem to vanish at dawn." Tony yanked up another blade of grass.

"Except who killed Cock Robin," he blurted. "And a few other unanswered questions, like how did Mrs. Robin get that yellow fabric?"

"Well, that's an easy one," Mary Alice said. "A box fell off the truck as it went to the dump and snips of the test fabric scattered along the Mayor's hedge. Sam helped the driver put it back . . . all but two pieces. He knew robins like to decorate their nests and threw them on the lawn for Mrs. R. She found one and the other must have blown into the hedge in that thunderstorm."

Tony smiled, partly because the answer was so simple, partly because Mary Alice still sounded like a lady of the manor, but a manor that had changed to a flower-rimmed cottage. She even had grass in her hair.

Rob was tapping his feet.

"You know," he said, "we're stuck because we haven't looked beyond Saddleboro for that last killer. The air flows over the entire world. What people do in

Who Really Did Kill Cock Robin?

Saddleboro affects the people in New York, Madrid, the Arctic, and the South Seas. And what they do affects us. The Earth is one ecosystem.

"Now everybody think!"

"Florida!" said Mary Alice. "Of course, the sparrow killed Cock Robin!"

"Sparrow!" said Tony incredulously. "What sparrow?"

"You know, the old nursery rhyme: '*Who killed Cock Robin? "I," said the Sparrow, "With my bow and arrow, I killed Cock Robin."* ' "

"Nuts," said Tony. "I thought you had something."

"I do! Where's that newspaper clipping I gave you?"

Tony stared at her. "Where is it? I never took it."

Mary Alice jumped up, ran across the Commons and down Maple. She returned a few minutes later and handed the clipping to Tony. "Here!" she exclaimed.

"By golly, she's right." He handed it to Rob. "It *is* the sparrow. Read it aloud."

" 'Homestead, Florida,' " Rob began. " 'Ten thousand birds were killed in a field near here when they ate seeds treated with mercurial compounds. The birds killed were primarily Savannah sparrows migrating north.'

"Doesn't help much," Rob said. "It's still the minor villain, mercury."

"Read on."

" 'The U.S. Department of Agriculture has now banned the use of the mercurial treatment of seeds. However, the disaster has had a chain effect. When the sparrows died millions of parasitic flies left their bodies. These attacked the next wave of the bird migration, which was largely thrushes.

" 'Since these parasites suck the blood of birds, many thrushes were weakened and died along the migration route.' "

"Oh, phooey," Mary Alice said. "The sparrow bugs killed thrushes, not robins."

"Robins *are* thrushes," Tony said as Rob snapped his fingers and stood up.

"How are we going to prove it was a parasite?" he asked. "I've destroyed the evidence. I kept only the tissues, not the skin where the bites would be." He clasped his hands behind his back and paced before the fountain. "Never thought of looking at the skin to see if it had marks on it. That's what you get for specializing—interest blindness. The case will never be closed."

Tony opened his notebook, turned to the second page, and found what he was looking for.

"Hold on, Rob. Listen to this.

" 'Friday, April 24, 6:10 A.M. Cock Robin is on his back. He is dead. Must be. Flylike insects with glassy wings are creeping off his body like rats abandoning a sinking ship.' "

"That's it! That's it. I'm satisfied." He grasped his hands with a clap and raised them above his head.

"DDT, PCB, MERCURY—AND THE SPAR-ROW WHO RELEASED THE PARASITIC ARROW."

Mayor Joe jumped to his feet. "DAVE! GET UP!"
Dave came sleepily to the window.

"QUIET!"

"I KNOW WHO KILLED COCK ROBIN."

"Who?"

"THE SPARROW, OF COURSE."

"I'll be right down." The Mayor hurried across the
street to the *Patent Reader* office and Mary Alice looked
admiringly at Tony.

"You're great!" she said. "Keeping all those careful
notes."

"Aw, come on," he said. "I'm not great. A team of
people killed Cock Robin and a team of people solved
the crime. And that's how it's going to be from now
until the day we live in balance with all beasts and
plants, and air and water."

"Let's fish!" said Mary Alice and went skipping across
the Commons toward Elm Street.

JEAN GEORGE was born in Washington, D.C., and was raised in a family of naturalists. Her father, an entomologist for the Department of Agriculture, and her twin brothers, now ecologists, introduced her to wildlife and nature, taking her with them into the wilderness to learn the plants and animals and their habitats and niches. She paddled canoes, hiked trails, built beds of boughs, and cooked wild foods.

Mrs. George was inspired to write this book by a little girl who brought a dying robin to her door and asked what was wrong with it. The author, who sees all of nature as a mystery, became more and more involved in tracking down the elusive killer. She modeled "Saddleboro" after a real town that she observed as it struggled with its own ecology problems.

In addition to being the author of many distinguished books for young people, Mrs. George has painted, danced, and written poetry. A former staff member of the *Washington Post*, she has participated in a bird study in Michigan and has raised bluejays, robins, and racoons. She is the mother of three wildlife enthusiasts and is a resident of Chappaqua, New York.